#169267

D1457546

1601,

AND

IS SHAKESPEARE DEAD?

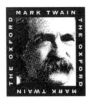

THE OXFORD MARK TWAIN

Shelley Fisher Fishkin, Editor

1601,

and

Is Shakespeare Dead?

Mark Twain

FOREWORD

SHELLEY FISHER FISHKIN

INTRODUCTION

ERICA JONG

AFTERWORD

LESLIE A. FIEDLER

New York   Oxford

OXFORD UNIVERSITY PRESS

1996

OXFORD UNIVERSITY PRESS

Oxford   New York

Athens, Auckland, Bangkok, Bogotá, Bombay
Buenos Aires, Calcutta, Cape Town, Dar es Salaam
Delhi, Florence, Hong Kong, Istanbul, Karachi
Kuala Lumpur, Madras, Madrid, Melbourne
Mexico City, Nairobi, Paris, Singapore
Taipei, Tokyo, Toronto
and associated companies in
Berlin, Ibadan

Copyright © 1996 by
Oxford University Press, Inc.
Introduction © 1996 by Erica Jong
Afterword © 1996 by Leslie A. Fiedler
Text design by Richard Hendel
Composition: David Thorne

Published by
Oxford University Press, Inc.
198 Madison Avenue, New York,
New York 10016

Oxford is a registered trademark of
Oxford University Press

Library of Congress
Cataloging-in-Publication Data

Twain, Mark, 1835–1910.
1601; and, Is Shakespeare dead? / by Mark Twain;
with an introduction by Erica Jong and an afterword
by Leslie A. Fiedler.
p. cm. — (The Oxford Mark Twain)
Includes bibliographical references.
Contents: Date, 1601: conversation, as it was by
the social fireside, in the time of the Tudors (1882) |
Is Shakespeare dead? (1909).
1. Raleigh, Walter, Sir, 1552?–1618—Fiction. 2. Great
Britain—History—Elizabeth, 1558–1603—Fiction.
3. Imaginary conversations. 4. Shakespeare, William,
1564–1616—Authorship—Baconian theory. I. Twain,
Mark, 1835–1910. Is Shakespeare dead? II. Title.
III. Title: Is Shakespeare dead? IV. Series Twain,
Mark, 1835–1910. Works. 1996.
PS1322.S45 1996
813'.4—dc20
96-15439
CIP
ISBN 0-19-510160-x (trade ed.)
ISBN 0-19-511426-4 (lib. ed.)
ISBN 0-19-509088-8 (trade ed. set)
ISBN 0-19-511345-4 (lib. ed. set)

9 8 7 6 5 4 3 2 1

Printed in the United States of America
on acid-free paper

FRONTISPIECE
Samuel L. Clemens poses here before the fireplace at
"Stormfield," his home in Redding, Connecticut, in
1909, the year he published *Is Shakespeare Dead?*
(The Mark Twain House, Hartford, Connecticut)

CONTENTS

EDITOR'S NOTE

The Oxford Mark Twain consists of twenty-nine volumes of facsimiles of the first American editions of Mark Twain's works, with an editor's foreword, new introductions, afterwords, notes on the texts, and essays on the illustrations in volumes with artwork. The facsimiles have been reproduced from the originals unaltered, except that blank pages in the front and back of the books have been omitted, and any seriously damaged or missing pages have been replaced by pages from other first editions (as indicated in the notes on the texts).

In the foreword, introduction, afterword, and essays on the illustrations, the titles of Mark Twain's works have been capitalized according to modern conventions, as have the names of characters (except where otherwise indicated). In the case of discrepancies between the title of a short story, essay, or sketch as it appears in the original table of contents and as it appears on its own title page, the title page has been followed. The parenthetical numbers in the introduction, afterwords, and illustration essays are page references to the facsimiles.

FOREWORD

Shelley Fisher Fishkin

Samuel Clemens entered the world and left it with Halley's Comet, little dreaming that generations hence Halley's Comet would be less famous than Mark Twain. He has been called the American Cervantes, our Homer, our Tolstoy, our Shakespeare, our Rabelais. Ernest Hemingway maintained that "all modern American literature comes from one book by Mark Twain called *Huckleberry Finn*." President Franklin Delano Roosevelt got the phrase "New Deal" from *A Connecticut Yankee in King Arthur's Court*. *The Gilded Age* gave an entire era its name. "The future historian of America," wrote George Bernard Shaw to Samuel Clemens, "will find your works as indispensable to him as a French historian finds the political tracts of Voltaire."[1]

There is a Mark Twain Bank in St. Louis, a Mark Twain Diner in Jackson Heights, New York, a Mark Twain Smoke Shop in Lakeland, Florida. There are Mark Twain Elementary Schools in Albuquerque, Dayton, Seattle, and Sioux Falls. Mark Twain's image peers at us from advertisements for Bass Ale (his drink of choice was Scotch), for a gas company in Tennessee, a hotel in the nation's capital, a cemetery in California.

Ubiquitous though his name and image may be, Mark Twain is in no danger of becoming a petrified icon. On the contrary: Mark Twain lives. *Huckleberry Finn* is "the most taught novel, most taught long work, and most taught piece of American literature" in American schools from junior high to the graduate level.[2] Hundreds of Twain impersonators appear in theaters, trade shows, and shopping centers in every region of the country.[3] Scholars publish hundreds of articles as well as books about Twain every year, and he is the subject of daily exchanges on the Internet. A journalist somewhere in the world finds a reason to quote Twain just about every day. Television series such as *Bonanza, Star Trek: The Next Generation,* and *Cheers* broadcast episodes that feature Mark Twain as a character. Hollywood screenwriters regularly produce movies inspired by his works, and writers of mysteries and science fiction continue to weave him into their plots.[4]

A century after the American Revolution sent shock waves throughout Europe, it took Mark Twain to explain to Europeans and to his countrymen alike what that revolution had wrought. He probed the significance of this new land and its new citizens, and identified what it was in the Old World that America abolished and rejected. The founding fathers had thought through the political dimensions of making a new society; Mark Twain took on the challenge of interpreting the social and cultural life of the United States for those outside its borders as well as for those who were living the changes he discerned.

Americans may have constructed a new society in the eighteenth century, but they articulated what they had done in voices that were largely inter-changeable with those of Englishmen until well into the nineteenth century. Mark Twain became the voice of the new land, the leading translator of what and who the "American" was — and, to a large extent, is. Frances Trollope's *Domestic Manners of the Americans,* a best-seller in England, Hector St. John de Crèvecoeur's *Letters from an American Farmer,* and Tocqueville's *Democracy in America* all tried to explain America to Europeans. But Twain did more than that: he allowed European readers to *experience* this strange "new world." And he gave his countrymen the tools to do two things they had not quite had the confidence to do before. He helped them stand before the cultural icons of the Old World unembarrassed, unashamed of America's lack of palaces and shrines, proud of its brash practicality and bold inventiveness, unafraid to reject European models of "civilization" as tainted or corrupt. And he also helped them recognize their own insularity, boorishness, arrogance, or ignorance, and laugh at it — the first step toward transcending it and becoming more "civilized," in the best European sense of the word.

Twain often strikes us as more a creature of our time than of his. He appreciated the importance and the complexity of mass tourism and public relations, fields that would come into their own in the twentieth century but were only fledgling enterprises in the nineteenth. He explored the liberating potential of humor and the dynamics of friendship, parenting, and marriage. He narrowed the gap between "popular" and "high" culture, and he meditated on the enigmas of personal and national identity. Indeed, it would be difficult to find an issue on the horizon today that Twain did not touch on somewhere in his work. Heredity versus environment? Animal rights? The boundaries of gender? The place of black voices in the cultural heritage of the United States? Twain was there.

With startling prescience and characteristic grace and wit, he zeroed in on many of the key challenges — political, social, and technological — that would face his country and the world for the next hundred years: the challenge of race relations in a society founded on both chattel slavery and ideals of equality, and the intractable problem of racism in American life; the potential of new technologies to transform our lives in ways that can be both exhilarating and terrifying — as well as unpredictable; the problem of imperialism and the difficulties entailed in getting rid of it. But he never lost sight of the most basic challenge of all: each man or woman's struggle for integrity in the face of the seductions of power, status, and material things.

Mark Twain's unerring sense of the right word and not its second cousin taught people to pay attention when he spoke, in person or in print. He said things that were smart and things that were wise, and he said them incomparably well. He defined the rhythms of our prose and the contours of our moral map. He saw our best and our worst, our extravagant promise and our stunning failures, our comic foibles and our tragic flaws. Throughout the world he is viewed as the most distinctively American of American authors — and as one of the most universal. He is assigned in classrooms in Naples, Riyadh, Belfast, and Beijing, and has been a major influence on twentieth-century writers from Argentina to Nigeria to Japan. The Oxford Mark Twain celebrates the versatility and vitality of this remarkable writer.

The Oxford Mark Twain reproduces the first American editions of Mark Twain's books published during his lifetime.[5] By encountering Twain's works in their original format — typography, layout, order of contents, and illustrations — readers today can come a few steps closer to the literary artifacts that entranced and excited readers when the books first appeared. Twain approved of and to a greater or lesser degree supervised the publication of all of this material.[6] The Mark Twain House in Hartford, Connecticut, generously loaned us its originals.[7] When more than one copy of a first American edition was available, Robert H. Hirst, general editor of the Mark Twain Project, in cooperation with Marianne Curling, curator of the Mark Twain House (and Jeffrey Kaimowitz, head of Rare Books for the Watkinson Library of Trinity College, Hartford, where the Mark Twain House collection is kept), guided our decision about which one to use.[8] As a set, the volumes also contain more than eighty essays commissioned especially for The Oxford Mark Twain, in which distinguished contributors reassess Twain's achievement as a writer and his place in the cultural conversation that he did so much to shape.

Each volume of The Oxford Mark Twain is introduced by a leading American, Canadian, or British writer who responds to Twain — often in a very personal way — as a fellow writer. Novelists, journalists, humorists, columnists, fabulists, poets, playwrights — these writers tell us what Twain taught them and what in his work continues to speak to them. Reading Twain's books, both famous and obscure, they reflect on the genesis of his art and the characteristics of his style, the themes he illuminated, and the aesthetic strategies he pioneered. Individually and collectively their contributions testify to the place Mark Twain holds in the hearts of readers of all kinds and temperaments.

Scholars whose work has shaped our view of Twain in the academy today have written afterwords to each volume, with suggestions for further reading. Their essays give us a sense of what was going on in Twain's life when he wrote the book at hand, and of how that book fits into his career. They explore how each book reflects and refracts contemporary events, and they show Twain responding to literary and social currents of the day, variously accepting, amplifying, modifying, and challenging prevailing paradigms. Sometimes they argue that works previously dismissed as quirky or eccentric departures actually address themes at the heart of Twain's work from the start. And as they bring new perspectives to Twain's composition strategies in familiar texts, several scholars see experiments in form where others saw only formlessness, method where prior critics saw only madness. In addition to elucidating the work's historical and cultural context, the afterwords provide an overview of responses to each book from its first appearance to the present.

Most of Mark Twain's books involved more than Mark Twain's words: unique illustrations. The parodic visual send-ups of "high culture" that Twain himself drew for *A Tramp Abroad*, the sketch of financial manipulator Jay Gould as a greedy and sadistic "Slave Driver" in *A Connecticut Yankee in King Arthur's Court*, and the memorable drawings of Eve in *Eve's Diary* all helped Twain's books to be sold, read, discussed, and preserved. In their essays for each volume that contains artwork, Beverly R. David and Ray Sapirstein highlight the significance of the sketches, engravings, and photographs in the first American editions of Mark Twain's works, and tell us what is known about the public response to them.

The Oxford Mark Twain invites us to read some relatively neglected works by Twain in the company of some of the most engaging literary figures of our time. Roy Blount Jr., for example, riffs in a deliciously Twain-like manner on "An Item Which the Editor Himself Could Not Understand," which may well rank as one of the least-known pieces Twain ever published. Bobbie Ann Mason celebrates the "mad energy" of Twain's most obscure comic novel, *The American Claimant*, in which the humor "hurtles beyond tall tale into simon-pure absurdity."[9] Garry Wills finds that *Christian Science* "gets us very close to the heart of American culture." Lee Smith reads "Political Economy" as a sharp and funny essay on language. Walter Mosley sees "The Stolen White Elephant," a story "reduced to a series of ridiculous telegrams related by an untrustworthy narrator caught up in an adventure that is as impossible as it is ludicrous," as a stunningly compact and economical satire of a world we still recognize as our own. Anne Bernays returns to "The Private History of a Campaign That Failed" and finds "an antiwar manifesto that is also confession, dramatic monologue, a plea for understanding and absolution, and a romp that gradually turns into atrocity even as we watch." After revisiting Captain Stormfield's heaven, Frederik Pohl finds that there "is no imaginable place more pleasant to spend eternity." Indeed, Pohl writes, "one would almost be willing to die to enter it."

While less familiar works receive fresh attention in The Oxford Mark Twain, new light is cast on the best-known works as well. Judith Martin ("Miss Manners") points out that it is by reading a court etiquette book that Twain's pauper learns how to behave as a proper prince. As important as etiquette may be in the palace, Martin notes, it is even more important in the slums.

> That etiquette is a sorer point with the ruffians in the street than with the proud dignitaries of the prince's court may surprise some readers. As in our own streets, etiquette is always a more volatile subject among those who cannot count on being treated with respect than among those who have the power to command deference.

And taking a fresh look at *Adventures of Huckleberry Finn*, Toni Morrison writes,

> much of the novel's genius lies in its quiescence, the silences that pervade it and give it a porous quality that is by turns brooding and soothing. It lies in . . . the subdued images in which the repetition of a simple word, such as "lonesome," tolls like an evening bell; the moments when nothing is said, when scenes and incidents swell the heart unbearably precisely because unarticulated, and force an act of imagination almost against the will.

Engaging Mark Twain as one writer to another, several contributors to The Oxford Mark Twain offer new insights into the processes by which his books came to be. Russell Banks, for example, reads *A Tramp Abroad* as "an important revision of Twain's incomplete first draft of *Huckleberry Finn*, a second draft, if you will, which in turn made possible the third and final draft." Erica Jong suggests that *1601*, a freewheeling parody of Elizabethan manners and mores, written during the same summer Twain began *Huckleberry Finn*, served as "a warm-up for his creative process" and "primed the pump for other sorts of freedom of expression." And Justin Kaplan suggests that "one of the transcendent figures standing behind and shaping" *Joan of Arc* was Ulysses S. Grant, whose memoirs Twain had recently published, and who, like Joan, had risen unpredictably "from humble and obscure origins" to become a "military genius" endowed with "the gift of command, a natural eloquence, and an equally natural reserve."

As a number of contributors note, Twain was a man ahead of his times. *The Gilded Age* was the first "Washington novel," Ward Just tells us, because "Twain was the first to see the possibilities that had eluded so many others." Commenting on *The Tragedy of Pudd'nhead Wilson,* Sherley Anne Williams observes that "Twain's argument about the power of environment in shaping character runs directly counter to prevailing sentiment where the negro was concerned." Twain's fictional technology, wildly fanciful by the standards of his day, predicts developments we take for granted in ours. DNA cloning, fax machines, and photocopiers are all prefigured, Bobbie Ann Mason tells us, in *The American Claimant.* Cynthia Ozick points out that the "telelectrophonoscope" we meet in "From the 'London Times' of 1904" is suspiciously like what we know as "television." And Malcolm Bradbury suggests that in the "phrenophones" of "Mental Telegraphy" "the Internet was born."

Twain turns out to have been remarkably prescient about political affairs as well. Kurt Vonnegut sees in *A Connecticut Yankee* a chilling foreshadowing (or perhaps a projection from the Civil War) of "all the high-tech atrocities which followed, and which follow still." Cynthia Ozick suggests that "The Man That Corrupted Hadleyburg," along with some of the other pieces collected under that title — many of them written when Twain lived in a Vienna ruled by Karl Lueger, a demagogue Adolf Hitler would later idolize — shoot up moral flares that shed an eerie light on the insidious corruption, prejudice, and hatred that reached bitter fruition under the Third Reich. And Twain's portrait in this book of "the dissolving Austria-Hungary of the 1890s," in Ozick's view, presages not only the Sarajevo that would erupt in 1914 but also "the disintegrated components of the former Yugoslavia" and "the *fin-de-siècle* Sarajevo of our own moment."

Despite their admiration for Twain's ambitious reach and scope, contributors to The Oxford Mark Twain also recognize his limitations. Mordecai Richler, for example, thinks that "the early pages of *Innocents Abroad* suffer from being a tad broad, proffering more burlesque than inspired satire," perhaps because Twain was "trying too hard for knee-slappers." Charles Johnson notes that the Young Man in Twain's philosophical dialogue about free will and determinism (*What Is Man?*) "caves in far too soon," failing to challenge what through late-twentieth-century eyes looks like "pseudoscience" and suspect essentialism in the Old Man's arguments.

Some contributors revisit their first encounters with Twain's works, recalling what surprised or intrigued them. When David Bradley came across "Fenimore Cooper's Literary Offences" in his college library, he "did not at first realize that Twain was being his usual ironic self with all this business about the 'nineteen rules governing literary art in the domain of romantic fiction,' but by the time I figured out there was no such list outside Twain's own head, I had decided that the rules made *sense*. . . . It seemed to me they were a pretty good blueprint for writing — Negro writing included." Sherley Anne Williams remembers that part of what attracted her to *Pudd'nhead Wilson* when she first read it thirty years ago was "that Twain, writing at the end of the nineteenth century, could imagine negroes as characters, albeit white ones, who actually thought for and of themselves, whose actions were the product of their thinking rather than the spontaneous ephemera of physical instincts that stereotype assigned to blacks." Frederik Pohl recalls his first reading of *Huckleberry Finn* as "a watershed event" in his life, the first book he read as a child in which "bad people" ceased to exercise a monopoly on doing "bad things." In *Huckleberry Finn* "some seriously bad things — things like the possession and mistreatment of black slaves, like stealing and lying, even like killing other people in duels — were quite often done by people who not only thought of themselves as exemplarily moral but, by any other standards I knew how to apply, actually *were* admirable citizens." The world that

Tom and Huck lived in, Pohl writes, "was filled with complexities and contradictions," and resembled "the world I appeared to be living in myself."

Other contributors explore their more recent encounters with Twain, explaining why they have revised their initial responses to his work. For Toni Morrison, parts of *Huckleberry Finn* that she "once took to be deliberate evasions, stumbles even, or a writer's impatience with his or her material," now strike her "as otherwise: as entrances, crevices, gaps, seductive invitations flashing the possibility of meaning. Unarticulated eddies that encourage diving into the novel's undertow — the real place where writer captures reader." One such "eddy" is the imprisonment of Jim on the Phelps farm. Instead of dismissing this portion of the book as authorial bungling, as she once did, Morrison now reads it as Twain's commentary on the 1880s, a period that "saw the collapse of civil rights for blacks," a time when "the nation, as well as Tom Sawyer, was deferring Jim's freedom in agonizing play." Morrison believes that Americans in the 1880s were attempting "to bury the combustible issues Twain raised in his novel," and that those who try to kick Huck Finn out of school in the 1990s are doing the same: "The cyclical attempts to remove the novel from classrooms extend Jim's captivity on into each generation of readers."

Although imitation-Hemingway and imitation-Faulkner writing contests draw hundreds of entries annually, no one has ever tried to mount a faux-Twain competition. Why? Perhaps because Mark Twain's voice is too much a part of who we are and how we speak even today. Roy Blount Jr. suggests that it is impossible, "at least for an American writer, to parody Mark Twain. It would be like doing an impression of your father or mother: he or she is already there in your voice."

Twain's style is examined and celebrated in The Oxford Mark Twain by fellow writers who themselves have struggled with the nuances of words, the structure of sentences, the subtleties of point of view, and the trickiness of opening lines. Bobbie Ann Mason observes, for example, that "Twain loved the sound of words and he knew how to string them by sound, like different shades of one color: 'The earl's barbaric eye,' 'the Usurping Earl,' 'a double-dyed humbug.'" Twain "relied on the punch of plain words" to show writers how to move beyond the "wordy romantic rubbish" so prevalent in nineteenth-century fiction, Mason says; he "was one of the first writers in America to deflower literary language." Lee Smith believes that "American writers have benefited as much from the way Mark Twain opened up the possibilities of first-person narration as we have from his use of vernacular language." (She feels that "the ghost of Mark Twain was hovering someplace in the background" when she decided to write her novel *Oral History* from the standpoint of multiple first-person narrators.) Frederick Busch maintains that "A Dog's Tale" "boasts one of the great opening sentences" of all time: "My father was a St. Bernard, my mother was a collie, but I am a Presbyterian." And Ursula Le Guin marvels at the ingenuity of the following sentence that she encounters in *Extracts from Adam's Diary*.

... This made her sorry for the creatures which live in there, which she calls fish, for she continues to fasten names on to things that don't need them and don't come when they are called by them, which is a matter of no consequence to her, as she is such a numskull anyway; so she got a lot of them out and brought them in last night and put them in my bed to keep warm, but I have noticed them now and then all day, and I don't see that they are any happier there than they were before, only quieter.[10]

Le Guin responds,

Now, that is a pure Mark-Twain-tour-de-force sentence, covering an immense amount of territory in an effortless, aimless ramble that seems to be heading nowhere in particular and ends up with breathtaking accuracy at the gold mine. Any sensible child would find that funny, perhaps not following all its divagations but delighted by the swing of it, by the word "numskull," by the idea of putting fish in the bed; and as that child grew older and reread it, its reward would only grow; and if that grown-up child had to write an essay on the piece and therefore earnestly studied and pored over this sentence, she would end up in unmitigated admiration of its vocabulary, syntax, pacing, sense, and rhythm, above all the beautiful timing of the last two words; and she would, and she does, still find it funny.

The fish surface again in a passage that Gore Vidal calls to our attention, from *Following the Equator*: "'The Whites always mean well when they take human fish out of the ocean and try to make them dry and warm and happy and comfortable in a chicken coop,' which is how, through civilization, they did away with many of the original inhabitants. Lack of empathy is a principal theme in Twain's meditations on race and empire."

Indeed, empathy — and its lack — is a principal theme in virtually all of Twain's work, as contributors frequently note. Nat Hentoff quotes the following thoughts from Huck in *Tom Sawyer Abroad*:

> I see a bird setting on a dead limb of a high tree, singing with its head tilted back and its mouth open, and before I thought I fired, and his song stopped and he fell straight down from the limb, all limp like a rag, and I run and picked him up and he was dead, and his body was warm in my hand, and his head rolled about this way and that, like his neck was broke, and there was a little white skin over his eyes, and one little drop of blood on the side of his head; and laws! I could n't see nothing more for the tears; and I hain't never murdered no creature since that war n't doing me no harm, and I ain't going to.[11]

"The Humane Society," Hentoff writes, "has yet to say anything as powerful — and lasting."

Readers of The Oxford Mark Twain will have the pleasure of revisiting Twain's Mississippi landmarks alongside Willie Morris, whose own lower Mississippi Valley boyhood gives him a special sense of connection to Twain. Morris knows firsthand the mosquitoes described in *Life on the Mississippi* — so colossal that "two of them could whip a dog" and "four of them could hold a man down"; in Morris's own hometown they were so large during the flood season that "local wags said they wore wristwatches." Morris's Yazoo City and Twain's Hannibal shared a "rough-hewn democracy . . . complicated by all the visible textures of caste and class, . . . harmless boyhood fun and mischief right along with . . . rank hypocrisies, churchgoing sanctimonies, racial hatred, entrenched and unrepentant greed."

For the West of Mark Twain's *Roughing It*, readers will have George Plimpton as their guide. "What a group these newspapermen were!" Plimpton writes about Twain and his friends Dan De Quille and Joe Goodman in Virginia City, Nevada. "Their roisterous carryings-on bring to mind the kind of frat-house enthusiasm one associates with college humor magazines like the *Harvard Lampoon*." Malcolm Bradbury examines Twain as "a living example of what made the American so different from the European." And Hal Holbrook, who has interpreted Mark Twain on stage for some forty years, describes how Twain "played" during the civil rights movement, during the Vietnam War, during the Gulf War, and in Prague on the eve of the demise of Communism.

Why do we continue to read Mark Twain? What draws us to him? His wit? His compassion? His humor? His bravura? His humility? His understanding of who and what we are in those parts of our being that we rarely open to view? Our sense that he knows we can do better than we do? Our sense that he knows we can't? E. L. Doctorow tells us that children are attracted to *Tom Sawyer* because in this book "the young reader confirms his own hope that no matter how troubled his relations with his elders may be, beneath all their disapproval is their underlying love for him, constant and steadfast." Readers in general, Arthur Miller writes, value Twain's "insights into America's always uncertain moral life and its shifting but everlasting hypocrisies"; we appreciate the fact that he "is not using his alienation from the public illusions of his hour in order to reject the country implicitly as though he could live without it, but manifestly in order to correct it." Perhaps we keep reading Mark Twain because, in Miller's words, he "wrote much more like a father than a son. He doesn't seem to be sitting in class taunting the teacher but standing at the head of it challenging his students to acknowledge their own humanity, that is, their immemorial attraction to the untrue."

Mark Twain entered the public eye at a time when many of his countrymen considered "American culture" an oxymoron; he died four years before a world conflagration that would lead many to question whether the contradiction in terms was not "European civilization" instead. In between he worked in journalism, printing, steamboating, mining, lecturing, publishing, and editing, in virtually every region of the country. He tried his hand at humorous sketches, social satire, historical novels, children's books, poetry, drama, science fiction, mysteries, romance, philosophy, travelogue, memoir, polemic, and several genres no one had ever seen before or has ever seen since. He invented a self-pasting scrapbook, a history game, a vest strap, and a gizmo for keeping bed sheets tucked in; he invested in machines and processes designed to revolutionize typesetting and engraving, and in a food supplement called "Plasmon." Along the way he cheerfully impersonated himself and prior versions of himself for doting publics on five continents while playing out a charming rags-to-riches story followed by a devastating riches-to-rags story followed by yet another great American comeback. He had a long-running real-life engagement in a sumptuous comedy of manners, and then in a real-life tragedy not of his own design: during the last fourteen years of his life almost everyone he ever loved was taken from him by disease and death.

Mark Twain has indelibly shaped our views of who and what the United States is as a nation and of who and what we might become. He understood the nostalgia for a "simpler" past that increased as that past receded — and he saw through the nostalgia to a past that was just as complex as the present. He recognized better than we did ourselves our potential for greatness and our potential for disaster. His fictions brilliantly illuminated the world in which he lived, changing it — and us — in the process. He knew that our feet often danced to tunes that had somehow remained beyond our hearing; with perfect pitch he played them back to us.

My mother read *Tom Sawyer* to me as a bedtime story when I was eleven. I thought Huck and Tom could be a lot of fun, but I dismissed Becky Thatcher as a bore. When I was twelve I invested a nickel at a local garage sale in a book that contained short pieces by Mark Twain. That was where I met Twain's Eve. Now, *that's* more like it, I decided, pleased to meet a female character I could identify *with* instead of against. Eve had spunk. Even if she got a lot wrong, you had to give her credit for trying. "The Man That Corrupted

Hadleyburg" left me giddy with satisfaction: none of my adolescent reveries of getting even with my enemies were half as neat as the plot of the man who got back at that town. "How I Edited an Agricultural Paper" set me off in uncontrollable giggles.

People sometimes told me that I looked like Huck Finn. "It's the freckles," they'd explain — not explaining anything at all. I didn't read *Huckleberry Finn* until junior year in high school in my English class. It was the fall of 1965. I was living in a small town in Connecticut. I expected a sequel to *Tom Sawyer*. So when the teacher handed out the books and announced our assignment, my jaw dropped: "Write a paper on how Mark Twain used irony to attack racism in *Huckleberry Finn*."

The year before, the bodies of three young men who had gone to Mississippi to help blacks register to vote — James Chaney, Andrew Goodman, and Michael Schwerner — had been found in a shallow grave; a group of white segregationists (the county sheriff among them) had been arrested in connection with the murders. America's inner cities were simmering with pent-up rage that began to explode in the summer of 1965, when riots in Watts left thirty-four people dead. None of this made any sense to me. I was confused, angry, certain that there was something missing from the news stories I read each day: the why. Then I met Pap Finn. And the Phelpses.

Pap Finn, Huck tells us, "had been drunk over in town" and "was just all mud." He erupts into a drunken tirade about "a free nigger . . . from Ohio — a mulatter, most as white as a white man," with "the whitest shirt on you ever see, too, and the shiniest hat; and there ain't a man in town that's got as fine clothes as what he had."

> . . . they said he was a p'fessor in a college, and could talk all kinds of languages, and knowed everything. And that ain't the wust. They said he could *vote*, when he was at home. Well, that let me out. Thinks I, what is the country a-coming to? It was 'lection day, and I was just about to go and vote, myself, if I warn't too drunk to get there; but when they told me there was a State in this country where they'd let that nigger vote, I drawed out. I says I'll never vote agin. Them's the very words I said. . . . And to see the

cool way of that nigger — why, he wouldn't a give me the road if I hadn't shoved him out o' the way.[12]

Later on in the novel, when the runaway slave Jim gives up his freedom to nurse a wounded Tom Sawyer, a white doctor testifies to the stunning altruism of his actions. The Phelpses and their neighbors, all fine, upstanding, well-meaning, churchgoing folk,

> agreed that Jim had acted very well, and was deserving to have some notice took of it, and reward. So every one of them promised, right out and hearty, that they wouldn't curse him no more.
>
> Then they come out and locked him up. I hoped they was going to say he could have one or two of the chains took off, because they was rotten heavy, or could have meat and greens with his bread and water, but they didn't think of it.[13]

Why did the behavior of these people tell me more about why Watts burned than anything I had read in the daily paper? And why did a drunk Pap Finn railing against a black college professor from Ohio whose vote was as good as his own tell me more about white anxiety over black political power than anything I had seen on the evening news?

Mark Twain knew that there was nothing, absolutely *nothing*, a black man could do — including selflessly sacrificing his freedom, the only thing of value he had — that would make white society see beyond the color of his skin. And Mark Twain knew that depicting racists with chilling accuracy would expose the viciousness of their world view like nothing else could. It was an insight echoed some eighty years after Mark Twain penned Pap Finn's rantings about the black professor, when Malcolm X famously asked, "Do you know what white racists call black Ph.D.'s?" and answered, "'*Nigger!*'"[14]

Mark Twain taught me things I needed to know. He taught me to understand the raw racism that lay behind what I saw on the evening news. He taught me that the most well-meaning people can be hurtful and myopic. He taught me to recognize the supreme irony of a country founded in freedom that continued to deny freedom to so many of its citizens. Every time I hear of another effort to kick Huck Finn out of school somewhere, I recall everything that Mark Twain taught *this* high school junior, and I find myself jumping into the fray.[15] I remember the black high school student who called CNN during the phone-in portion of a 1985 debate between Dr. John Wallace, a black educator spearheading efforts to ban the book, and myself. She accused Dr. Wallace of insulting her and all black high school students by suggesting they weren't smart enough to understand Mark Twain's irony. And I recall the black cameraman on the *CBS Morning News* who came up to me after he finished shooting another debate between Dr. Wallace and myself. He said he had never read the book by Mark Twain that we had been arguing about — but now he really wanted to. One thing that puzzled him, though, was why a white woman was defending it and a black man was attacking it, because as far as he could see from what we'd been saying, the book made whites look pretty bad.

As I came to understand *Huckleberry Finn* and *Pudd'nhead Wilson* as commentaries on the era now known as the nadir of American race relations, those books pointed me toward the world recorded in nineteenth-century black newspapers and periodicals and in fiction by Mark Twain's black contemporaries. My investigation of the role black voices and traditions played in shaping Mark Twain's art helped make me aware of their role in shaping all of American culture.[16] My research underlined for me the importance of changing the stories we tell about who we are to reflect the realities of what we've been.[17]

Ever since our encounter in high school English, Mark Twain has shown me the potential of American literature and American history to illuminate each other. Rarely have I found a contradiction or complexity we grapple with as a nation that Mark Twain had not puzzled over as well. He insisted on taking America seriously. And he insisted on *not* taking America seriously: "I think that there is but a single specialty with us, only one thing that can be called by the wide name 'American,'" he once wrote. "That is the national devotion to ice-water."[18]

Mark Twain threw back at us our dreams and our denial of those dreams, our greed, our goodness, our ambition, and our laziness, all rattling around together in that vast echo chamber of our talk — that sharp, spunky American talk that Mark Twain figured out how to write down without robbing it of its energy and immediacy. Talk shaped by voices that the official arbiters of "culture" deemed of no importance — voices of children, voices of slaves, voices of servants, voices of ordinary people. Mark Twain listened. And he made us listen. To the stories he told us, and to the truths they conveyed. He still has a lot to say that we need to hear.

Mark Twain lives — in our libraries, classrooms, homes, theaters, movie houses, streets, and most of all in our speech. His optimism energizes us, his despair sobers us, and his willingness to keep wrestling with the hilarious and horrendous complexities of it all keeps us coming back for more. As the twenty-first century approaches, may he continue to goad us, chasten us, delight us, berate us, and cause us to erupt in unrestrained laughter in unexpected places.

NOTES

1. Ernest Hemingway, *Green Hills of Africa* (New York: Charles Scribner's Sons, 1935), 22. George Bernard Shaw to Samuel L. Clemens, July 3, 1907, quoted in Albert Bigelow Paine, *Mark Twain: A Biography* (New York: Harper and Brothers, 1912), 3:1398.

2. Allen Carey-Webb, "Racism and *Huckleberry Finn*: Censorship, Dialogue and Change," *English Journal* 82, no. 7 (November 1993):22.

3. See Louis J. Budd, "Impersonators," in J. R. LeMaster and James D. Wilson, eds., *The Mark Twain Encyclopedia* (New York: Garland Publishing Company, 1993), 389–91.

4. See Shelley Fisher Fishkin, "Ripples and Reverberations," part 3 of *Lighting Out for the Territory: Reflections on Mark Twain and American Culture* (New York: Oxford University Press, 1996).

5. There are two exceptions. Twain published chapters from his autobiography in the *North American Review* in 1906 and 1907, but this material was not published in book form in Twain's lifetime; our volume reproduces the material as it appeared in the *North American Review*. The other exception is our final volume, *Mark Twain's Speeches*, which appeared two months after Twain's death in 1910.

An unauthorized handful of copies of *1601* was privately printed by an Alexander Gunn of Cleveland at the instigation of Twain's friend John Hay in 1880. The first American edition authorized by Mark Twain, however, was printed at the United States Military Academy at West Point in 1882; that is the edition reproduced here.

It should further be noted that four volumes — *The Stolen White Elephant and Other Detective Stories*, *Following the Equator and Anti-imperialist Essays*, *The Diaries of Adam and Eve*, and *1601, and Is Shakespeare Dead?*—bind together material originally published separately. In each case the first American edition of the material is the version that has been reproduced, always in its entirety. Because Twain constantly recycled and repackaged previously published works in his collections of short pieces, a certain amount of duplication is unavoidable. We have selected volumes with an eye toward keeping this duplication to a minimum.

Even the twenty-nine-volume Oxford Mark Twain has had to leave much out. No edition of Twain can ever claim to be "complete," for the man was too prolix, and the file drawers of both ephemera and as yet unpublished texts are deep.

6. With the possible exception of *Mark Twain's Speeches*. Some scholars suspect Twain knew about this book and may have helped shape it, although no hard evidence to that effect has yet surfaced. Twain's involvement in the production process varied greatly from book to book. For a fuller sense of authorial intention, scholars will continue to rely on the superb definitive editions of Twain's works produced by the Mark Twain Project at the University of California at Berkeley as they become available. Dense with annotation documenting textual emendation and related issues, these editions add immeasurably to our understanding of Mark Twain and the genesis of his works.

7. Except for a few titles that were not in its collection. The American Antiquarian Society in Worcester, Massachusetts, provided the first edition of *King Leopold's Soliloquy*; the Elmer Holmes Bobst Library of New York University furnished the 1906–7 volumes of the *North American Review* in which *Chapters from My Autobiography* first appeared; the Harry Ransom Humanities Research Center at the University of Texas at Austin made their copy of the West Point edition of *1601* available; and the Mark Twain Project provided the first edition of *Extract from Captain Stormfield's Visit to Heaven*.

8. The specific copy photographed for Oxford's facsimile edition is indicated in a note on the text at the end of each volume.

9. All quotations from contemporary writers in this essay are taken from their introductions to the volumes of The Oxford Mark Twain, and the quotations from Mark Twain's works are taken from the texts reproduced in The Oxford Mark Twain.

10. *The Diaries of Adam and Eve*, The Oxford Mark Twain [hereafter OMT] (New York: Oxford University Press, 1996), p. 33.

11. *Tom Sawyer Abroad*, OMT, p. 74.

12. *Adventures of Huckleberry Finn*, OMT, p. 49–50.

13. Ibid., p. 358.

14. Malcolm X, *The Autobiography of Malcolm X*, with the assistance of Alex Haley (New York: Grove Press, 1965), p. 284.

15. I do not mean to minimize the challenge of teaching this difficult novel, a challenge for which all teachers may not feel themselves prepared. Elsewhere I have developed some concrete strategies for approaching the book in the classroom, including teaching it in the context of the history of American race relations and alongside books by black writers. See Shelley Fisher Fishkin, "Teaching *Huckleberry Finn*," in James S. Leonard, ed., *Making Mark Twain Work in the Classroom* (Durham: Duke University Press, forthcoming). See also Shelley Fisher Fishkin, *Was Huck Black? Mark Twain and African-American Voices* (New York: Oxford University Press, 1993), pp. 106–8, and a curriculum kit in preparation at the Mark Twain House in Hartford, containing teaching suggestions from myself, David Bradley, Jocelyn Chadwick-Joshua, James Miller, and David E. E. Sloane.

16. See Fishkin, *Was Huck Black?* See also Fishkin, "Interrogating 'Whiteness,' Complicating 'Blackness': Remapping American Culture," in Henry Wonham, ed., *Criticism and the Color Line: Desegregating American Literary Studies* (New Brunswick: Rutgers UP, 1996, pp. 251–90 and in shortened form in *American Quarterly* 47, no. 3 (September 1995):428–66.

17. I explore the roots of my interest in Mark Twain and race at greater length in an essay entitled "Changing the Story," in Jeffrey Rubin-Dorsky and Shelley Fisher Fishkin, eds., *People of the Book: Thirty Scholars Reflect on Their Jewish Identity* (Madison: U of Wisconsin Press, 1996), pp. 47–63.

18. "What Paul Bourget Thinks of Us," *How to Tell a Story and Other Essays*, OMT, p. 197.

INTRODUCTION

1601 and *Is Shakespeare Dead?*
"Deliberate Lewdness" and
the Lure of Immortality

Erica Jong

The form of government most suitable to the artist is no government at all.
— *Oscar Wilde*

We live in a time when the freedom to publish sexual oriented material is coming under attack, when large publishing conglomerates increasingly control all means of communication, and when the forces of cultural reaction are becoming extremely well organized. The brief cultural *glasnost* of the sixties is beginning to seem quaint. At such a juncture it is particularly important to reexamine what constitutes forbidden material in literature and to cut through the political grandstanding about its supposed evils in order to understand what *purpose* it actually serves in society. If nothing else, we should try to grasp what motivates the creators and consumers of it.

Pornographic material has been present in the art and literature of every society in every historical period. What has changed from epoch to epoch — or even from one decade to another — is the degree to which such material has flourished publicly and been distributed legally. In elitist societies there are, paradoxically, fewer calls for censorship than in democratic ones, since elitist societies function as de facto censors, keeping certain materials out of the purview of *hoi polloi*. As democracy increases, so does the demand for legal control over the erotic, the pornographic, the scatological. Our own century is a perfect example of the oscillations of taste regarding such material. We have gone from the banning and burning of D. H. Lawrence, James Joyce, Radclyffe Hall, Henry Miller and other avant-garde artists early in the century to a passionate struggle to free literature from censorship in mid-century to a new wave of reaction at century's end.

After many brave battles for the freedom to publish, we find that the enemies of freedom have multiplied rather than diminished. They include Christians, Muslims, oppressive totalitarian regimes, even well-meaning social libertarians who happen to be feminists, teachers, members of school boards, librarians. This should not surprise us, since the demand for state censorship is usually "a response to the presence within the society of heterogeneous groups of people with differing standards and aspirations," as Margaret Mead pointed out forty years ago. As our culture becomes more diverse, we can expect more calls for censorship rather than fewer. So we owe it to ourselves to understand the impulses toward pornography, eroticism, scatology, before resuming our contentious public debate about their uses and whether or not they should be restricted.

Our job is made tougher and more confusing by the fact that the spate of freedoms we briefly enjoyed in the late sixties, the seventies and the early eighties led to the proliferation of sexual materials so ugly, exploitative and misogynistic that it is difficult to defend them. The door was opened to *Lolita, Lady Chatterley's Lover, Tropic of Cancer, Couples, Portnoy's Complaint, Fear of Flying*, but it was also opened to *Debbie Does Dallas, Deep Throat* and an array of printed and filmed pornography that is deeply offensive to women and has understandably provoked the ire of feminists. Pornography also became hugely profitable once legal restraints were lifted, which in turn gave rise to another wave of reaction.

We stand at a crossroads now when many former libertarians and liberals suddenly want to ban sexual materials. The old dream of the avant-garde that eradicating sexual oppression would free human beings from their inhibitions and limitations has withered. We think we are sadder and wiser about what sexual freedom leads to, but in truth we never really *tried* sexual freedom. We only ballyhooed its simulacrum.

I want to bypass a reappraisal of the so-called sexual revolution for the moment and look instead at the impulse to create pornography and the role it plays in one artist's oeuvre. I should say that I use the terms "pornography" and "eroticism" interchangeably because I have come to the conclusion that only snobbery divides them. At one time I thought of pornography as purely an aid to masturbation, and of eroticism as something more high-toned and spiritual, like Molly Bloom's soliloquy in *Ulysses*. Now I doubt that division. Nearly every visual artist — from the anonymous sculptor of the bare-breasted Minoan snake goddess to Pompeii's brothel muralists to John Ruskin and Pablo Picasso — has been drawn to the erotic and the pornographic. So have literary artists throughout human history. Sometimes the urge has been to stimulate the genitals; sometimes the urge has been to stimulate the mind. Since the mind and the genitals are part of one organism, why distinguish between masturbatory dreams and aesthetic ones? Surely there is also an aesthetic of masturbation that our society is too sex-negative to explore. At any rate, it is time to go back to the origin of the pornographic impulse and explore the reasons it is so tenacious.

Mark Twain's *1601* is a perfect place to start. Although Twain lived in the Victorian age and knew he could never publish his pornographic fancies officially, they nevertheless occupied his energies from time to time, and he was so proud of them that he sought to disseminate them among his friends. I will argue that in Mark Twain's case, pornography was an *essential* part of his oeuvre because it primed the pump for other sorts of freedom of expression. It allowed him to fly free in fashioning a new sort of American vernacular in first-person narratives that drew on American speech patterns and revealed the soul of America as never before. Experiments with pornography, scatology and eroticism helped him to delve into the communal unconscious and create some of the most profound myths of American culture.

The notorious *1601*, or *Conversation, As It Was by the Social Fireside, in the time of the Tudors*, fascinates me because it demonstrates how closely Mark

Twain's passion for linguistic experiment is allied with his compulsion toward "deliberate lewdness." The phase is Vladimir Nabokov's. In a witty afterword to *Lolita* (1955), he links the urge to create pornography with "the verve of a fine poet in a wanton mood" and regrets that "in modern times the term 'pornography' connotes mediocrity, commercialism, and certain strict rules of narration." In contemporary porn, Nabokov says, "action has to be limited to the copulation of clichés." Poetry is always out of the question. "Style, structure, imagery should never distract the reader from his tepid lust." Motivated by such lackluster lust, the connoisseur of pornography is impatient with all attempts at verbal dexterity and linguistic wit. One is reminded that Henry Miller failed miserably as a paid pornographer because he could not leave the poetry out as his anonymous patron wished. Anaïs Nin fared better with *Delta of Venus* and *Little Birds*. For Henry Miller pornography mattered precisely *because* it aroused him to poetry. Miller and Nabokov shared the ancient pagan attitude toward pornography. For them, "deliberate lewdness" was an exuberant literary strategy.

Poetry and pornography went hand in hand in Roman, Renaissance and eighteenth-century literature. The pornographic flights of Catullus, Ovid, Petronius and Juvenal never sacrificed style. Boccaccio, Villon, Rabelais, Cervantes, Shakespeare, John Donne and Andrew Marvell all delighted in making porn poetic. Jonathan Swift, Alexander Pope and Laurence Sterne were equally drunk with lewdness and with language.

No creator should have to bother about "the exact demarcation between the sensuous and the sensual," says Nabokov. Let the censors worry about such hypocritical distinctions. The literary artist has another agenda: to free the imagination and let the wildness of the mind take flight. Nabokov is, of course, defending his own offspring *Lolita*, that light of his loins and pen which caused such consternation that it could not at first be published anywhere but in Paris by Maurice Girodias's Olympia Press. The pornographic verve of ancient literature was Nabokov's inspiration: in this he would have recognized Mark Twain as a brother.

In choosing to write *1601* from the point of view of "the Pepys of that day, the same being cup-bearer to Queen Elizabeth," Mark Twain was transporting himself to a world that existed before the invention of sexual hypocrisy. The Elizabethans were openly bawdy. They found bodily functions funny and sex arousing to the muse. Restoration wits and Augustan satirists had the same openness to the body and the same respect for eros. Only in the nineteenth century did prudery (and the threat of legal censure) begin to paralyze the author's hand. Shakespeare, Rochester and Pope were far more fettered *politically* than we are, but they were not required to put condoms on their pens when the matter of sex arose. They were *pleased* to remind their readers of the essential messiness of the body. They followed a classical tradition that often expressed moral indignation through scatology. "Oh Celia, Celia, Celia shits," writes Swift, as if she were the first woman in history to do so. In his so-called unprintable poems, Swift is debunking the conventions of courtly love (as well as expressing his own deep misogny), but he is doing so in a spirit that Catullus and Juvenal would have recognized. The satirist lashes the world to bring the world to its senses. He does the dance of the satyrs around our follies.

Twain's scatology serves this purpose as well, but it is also a warm-up for his creative process. Stuck in the prudish nineteenth century, Mark Twain craved the freedom of the ancients. In championing "deliberate lewdness" in *1601*, he bestowed the gift of freedom on himself.

It is hardly coincidental that Mark Twain was writing *1601* during the same summer of 1876 when he was "tearing along on a new book" — the first sixteen chapters of a novel he then referred to as "Huck Finn's Autobiography." *1601* and *Adventures of Huckleberry Finn* have a great deal in common. According to Justin Kaplan, "Both were implicit rejections of the taboos and codes of polite society, and both were experiments in using the vernacular as a literary medium."

Is there a stronger connection between *Huckleberry Finn* and *1601*? As a professional writer whose process of composition often resembles Twain's (intermittent work on ambitious novels, writing blocks during which I put one project aside and devote myself to others, periods of lecturing and travel), I think I understand Twain's creative strategy. He was sneaking up on the muse so that she would not be forewarned and escape. Every author knows that a book only begins to live when the voice of its narrator comes alive. You may have plot ideas, characters may haunt you in the night, but the book does not fly until the sound of its voice is heard in the author's ear. And the sound of a book's voice is as individual as the sound of a child's voice. It may resemble that of other offspring, but it always has its own particular timbre, its own particular quirks.

In order to find the true voice of the book, the author must be free to play without fear of reprisal. All writing blocks come from excessive self-judgment, the internalized voice of the critical parent telling the author's imagination that it is a dirty little boy or girl. "Hah!" says the author. "I will flaunt the voice of parental propriety and break free!" This is why the pornographic spirit is *always* related to unhampered creativity. Artists are fascinated with filth because we know that in filth everything human is born. Human beings emerge between piss and shit, and so do novels and poems. Only by letting go of the inhibition that makes us bow to social propriety can we plumb the depths of the unconscious. We assert our freedom with pornographic play. If we are lucky, we *keep* that freedom long enough to create a masterpiece like *Huckleberry Finn*.

But the two compulsions are more than just related; they are *causally* intertwined. When *Huckleberry Finn* was published in 1885, Louisa May Alcott put her finger on exactly what mattered about the novel even as she condemned it: "If Mr. Clemens cannot think of something better to tell our pure-minded lads and lasses, he had best stop writing for them." What Alcott didn't know was that "our pure-minded lads and lasses" aren't. But Mark Twain knew. It is not at all surprising that during that summer of high scatological spirits Twain should also give birth to the irreverent voice of Huck. If *Little Women* fails to go as deep as Twain's masterpiece, it is precisely because of Alcott's concern with pure-mindedness. Niceness is ever the enemy of art. If you worry about what the neighbors, critics, parents and supposedly pure-minded censors think, you will never create a work that defies the restrictions of the conscious mind and delves into the world of dreams.

1601 is deliberately lewd. It delights in stinking up the air of propriety. It delights in describing great thunder-gusts of farts that make great stenches, and pricks that are stiff until cunts "take ye stiffness out of them" (ix). In the midst of all this ribaldry, the assembled company speaks of many things — poetry, theater, art, politics. Twain knew that the muse flies on the wings of flatus, and he was having such a good time writing this Elizabeth pastiche that the humor shines through a hundred years and twenty later. I dare you to read *1601* without giggling and guffawing.

In the last few years a great deal of pious politically correct garbage has been written about pornography. Pornography, the high-minded self-anointed feminist Catharine MacKinnon tell us, is tantamount to an assault on women and causes rape. Pornography, MacKinnon's comrade-in-arms Andrea Dworkin asserts, is a *form* of rape.

A chorus of younger feminists at last has come along to counter these dangerous unexamined contentions. Pornography, says Susie Bright, is necessary to liberation. Pornography, says Sallie Tisdale, is desired by women as well as men. Pornography, says Nadine Strossen, is guaranteed by the Bill of Rights.

But what about the Bill of Rights for artists? Could Robert Mapplethorpe's photographs of lilies have existed without his photographs of pricks? Could Henry Miller have grasped human transcendence in *The Colossus of Maroussi* without having wallowed in the sewers of Paris in *Tropic of Cancer*?

I say no. Without farts, there are no flowers. Without pricks, there are no poems.

This is not the first time in history we have seen an essentially libertarian movement like feminism devolve into a debate about pure-mindedness. The suffragists of the last century also turned into prudish prohibitionists who spent their force proscribing drink and policing morals. One might argue that a concern with pure-mindedness is fatal not only to art but also to political movements.

Why does this urge toward repression crop up in supposedly libertarian movements? And why does the puritanical drive to censor the artist keep recurring? The artist needs to be free to play in the id in order to bring back insights for the ego. But the id is scary. It yawns like a bottomless *vagina dentata*. It threatens to bite off heads, hands, cocks, and to swallow us up in

XXXVIII : ERICA JONG

our own darkest impulses. Society fears the id even as it yearns for the release to be found there. We retreat from dream and fantasy even as we long to submerge in them. Make no mistake about it: the primal ooze of creation *is* terrifying. It reminds us of how little control we have over our lives, over our deaths. It reminds us of our origins and inspires us to contemplate our inevitable annihilation.

Pornographic art is perceived as dangerous to political movements because, like the unconscious, it is not programmable. It is dangerous play whose outcome can never be predicted. Since dream is the speech of the unconscious, the artist who would create works of value must be fluent in the language of dream. The pornographic has a direct connection to the unconscious.

I suspect this was why Twain was having such fun with *1601* in the summer of 1876. The filth of *1601* fertilized the garden of Huck's adventures. Like any literary artist who is in touch with his id, Twain instinctively knew that sex and creativity were interrelated. He could not fill *Huckleberry Finn* with farts, pricks and cunts, but he could play in *1601* and prepare his imagination for the antisocial adventures he would give his antihero in the other book.

In his classic essay "Obscenity and the Law of Reflection," Henry Miller suggests that "when obscenity crops out in art, in literature more particularly, it usually functions as a technical device. . . . Its purpose is to awaken, to usher in a sense of reality. In a sense, its use by the artist may be compared to the use of the miraculous by the Masters." Here Miller means the *spiritual* masters. He believed that Christ and the Zen masters only resorted to miracles when such were absolutely necessary to awaken their disciples. The artist uses obscenity the same way. "The real nature of the obscene lies in its lust to convert," Miller says. Obscenity operates in literature as a sort of wake-up call to the unconscious. Obscenity transports us to "another dimension of reality."

Havelock Ellis once said that "adults need obscene literature, as much as children need fairy tales, as a relief from the obsessive force of convention." The urge toward obscenity is nothing more or less than the urge toward freedom. Those who condemn it are clearly afraid of the debauchery that freedom might unleash in them. They inevitably denounce what they are most attracted to. The censor is the one who slavers in private over books, films and visual artifacts that he or she then proscribes for the rest of society.

Throughout history, the urge to censor has always been strongest in those most attracted to the freedom of the obscene. In quashing freedom in others, the censor hopes to quash it within. "Liberation," says Henry Miller, "implies the sloughing off of chains, the bursting of the cocoon. What is obscene are the preliminary or anticipatory movements of birth, the preconscious writhing in the face of a life to be."

Miller goes on to say that the obscene "is an attempt to spy on the secret processes of the universe." The guilt of the creator when he or she knows that something extraordinary is being born comes from the knowledge of tampering with godlike powers, a Promethean guilt for impersonating the immortals. "The obscene has all the qualities of the hidden interval," Miller says. It is

vast as the Unconscious itself and as amorphous and fluid as the very stuff of the Unconscious. It is what comes to the surface as strange, intoxicating and forbidden, and which therefore arrests and paralyzes, when in the form of Narcissus we bend over our own image in the mirror of our own iniquity. Acknowledged by all, it is nevertheless despised and rejected, wherefore it is constantly emerging in Protean guise at the most unexpected moments. When it is recognized and accepted . . . it inspires no more dread than . . . the flowering lotus which sends its roots down into the mud of the stream on which it is borne.

Sexuality and creativity were not always divorced as they are today and as they were in Mark Twain's day. All so-called primitive and pagan art exhibits the marriage of sexuality and creativity, whether in the form of giant phalluses, multitudinous breasts or pregnant bellies. But the divorce between body and mind that characterizes the Christian era has led the artist to curious strategies of creation and constant guilt for the possession of the creative gift.

We see this guilt as clearly in Mark Twain as in any artist who ever lived. His creative strategies of intermittent composition, his fear of working on a book once it became clear that the writing would inevitably lift the veil and take him into the sacred and forbidden precincts, betray his hypersensitivity to something we might call post-Christian creator guilt, if it weren't such a mouthful.

In "primitive" societies, the artist and the shaman are one. There *is* no discontinuity between artistic creation and the sacred. The shaman-artist creates in order to worship and worships in order to create. Not so the artist in our culture. Always wracked by guilt for the power of creativity itself, beset by censors within and without, our artists are shackled by a sense of transgression so deep it often destroys them. No wonder we use obscenity to break open the door, to lift the veil. No wonder we insist on our right to do so as if our lives depended on it.

They do.

Shakespeare occupies a special place for writers who use the English language. He is at once touchstone, muse and role model. His work is so various that its author can be made to stand for just about anything. Dante in Italian literature and Pushkin in Russian literature are in some ways analogous figures to Shakespeare, but Pushkin is a closer fit because his irreverence and bawdiness are as beloved by Russians as his poetics.

It is Shakespeare's range that so amazes. He inspires us as the supreme maker of love poetry (the sonnets, *Romeo and Juliet*), as a political sage (the history plays), and as a deft psychologist (*Hamlet, Lear, Macbeth*). In addition, he can play the rumbustious clown who marries poetry with pornography, exalted language with the basest of subject matter.

Shakespeare claims his unique position in English literature because he is the poet of the demotic as well as the aristrocratic. He can range from slapstick comedy to elitist elegance with unsurpassed ease. Shakespeare's work is also infinitely open to parody, and Shakespearean parodies are more often than not acts of love. He is the first poet we know and the first among poets. We cut our teeth on him and are astounded to discover that he still delights when our teeth our falling out.

Mark Twain was powerfully attracted to Shakespeare, and to the Elizabethan licentiousness that fed his genius with the pure elixir of freedom. He made "Master Shakspur" a character in *1601*, had him disavow authorship of the "firmament-clogging" fart that opens the conversation, and reported (in the person of the cupbearer) his discourse on "ye custom of widows of Perigord to wear upon ye hedde-dress, in sign of widowhood, a jewel in ye similitude of a man's member wilted & limber," among other matters (v). He read Shakespeare's plays in preparation for writing *The Prince and the Pauper*, he wrote several Shakespearean burlesques, and he brought Shakespeare to the Mississippi in *Huckleberry Finn* in the persons of the Duke and the King.

But *Is Shakespeare Dead?*, Mark Twain's only book about another author, is an odd, confused work. It is more about Mark Twain than about William Shakespeare; indeed Twain *knows* this and bills it as a piece of his autobiography.

Shakespeare's largeness and diversity inspire envy and ambivalence in those who crawl between his huge legs as he bestrides English literature like a colossus. This was Mark Twain's reaction exactly. In *1601*, Twain both parodied and paid homage to Shakespeare's liberating bawdry. In *The Prince and the Pauper*, he entered Shakespeare's world and appropriated characters who might have been his. And in *Is Shakespeare Dead?* he tried to come to terms with his conflicting responses to Shakespeare as mentor and muse.

The pretext for the book is the old controversy between Stratfordians and Baconians, which was revived by the 1908 publication of George Greenwood's *The Shakespeare Problem Restated* and William Stone Booth's *Some Acrostic Signatures of Francis Bacon*, which Mark Twain read in proofs. But Twain is really concerned with his own impending death and his place in literary history. How fickle anyway is fame? If the greatest poet in our language is so unknown as a man, then what about *me*, Twain seems to ask. Since Twain identifies with Shakespeare, his musings on the poet's virtual disappearance from the world of facts is threatening because it may foreshadow his *own* disappearance. *Is Shakespeare Dead?* consists of disguised — and not so disguised — meditations on Twain's own chances for immortality as both an author and a character. Being a character sometimes seemed as important to Twain as being an author, so it is not surprising that was alarmed by the dearth of anecdotes about Shakespeare.

Twain argues that Shakespeare of Stratford could not have been the author of the plays and poems because, at his death, he was scarcely mentioned in his hometown. He further agues that the plays and poems are full of detailed legal knowledge reflecting an education that Shakespeare of Stratford could not have received. His parents, though mildly prosperous for a time, were illiterate, after all. And the one funeral quatrain with which he can be positively identified is a piece of embarrassing doggerel. Clearly, this Stratford bourgeois is not the poet of the sonnets and plays.

Do we believe this? Does Mark Twain? He seems to raise all these questions merely as an excuse to relate an anecdote that shows the extent of his own fame in his hometown of Hannibal and throughout the United States. He comes, in short, not to bury Shakespeare but to praise himself, and to put his writing hand out to be touched by the scepter of immortality.

We are left perplexed and unsatisfied by this book. It seems to have a hidden agenda. But what is that agenda? It is to prove that Twain is a greater celebrity than Shakespeare and therefore a greater writer? It is a sort of deathbed confession from a man who loved fame too much and knew it? Is it an attempt to discredit in advance the critical vultures who would rush in after Twain's death, proposing this, presuming that, theorizing about the roots of his genius? Above all, *Is Shakespeare Dead?* seems to be the *cri de coeur* of an aging author approaching death. *Here's what eternity did to the greatest poet who ever lived*, we hear him saying. *What will eternity do to me?*

1601

Date 1601.

CONVERSATION, AS IT WAS BY THE SOCIAL FIRESIDE,

IN THE TIME OF THE TUDORS.

[MEM.—The following is supposed to be an extract from the diary of the Pepys of that day, the same being cup-bearer to Queen Elizabeth. It is supposed that he is of ancient and noble lineage ; that he despises these literary *canaille ;* that his soul consumes with wrath to see the Queen stooping to talk with such ; and that the old man feels his nobility defiled by contact with Shakspere, etc., and yet he has *got* to stay there till Her Majesty chooses to dismiss him.]

YESTERNIGHT toke her maieſtie ẙ queene a fan-
taſie ſuch as ſhee ſometimes hath, & hadde to her
oſet certaine ẙ doe write playes, bookes, & ſvch
like, theſe beeing my lord Bacon, his worſhip Sr.
Walter Ralegh, Mr. Ben Jonſon, & ẙ childe Fran-
cɪs Beaumonte, wᶜʰ beeing but ſixteen, hath yet
urned his hãd to ẙ doing of ẙ Lattin maſters in-
o our Englyche tong, with grete diſcretion&much
applaus.   Alſo came with theſe ẙ famous Shaxpur.   A righte ſtraunge mixing truly of mighty
bloud with meã, ẙ more in eſpecial ſyns ẙ queenes
grace was preſent, as likewyſe theſe following, to
wit: Ye Ducheſſe of Bilgewater, twenty-two yeeres
of age ; ẙ Counteſſe of Granby, twenty-ſix ; her
doter, ẙ Lady Helen, fifteen ; as alſo theſe two
maides of honor, to wit : ẙ Lady MargeryBoothy,
ſixty-fiue, & ẙ Lady Alice Dilberry, turned ſeuen-
ty, ſhee beeing two yeeres ẙ queenes graces elder.
    I   beeing her mai^sty's cup-bearer, hadde no
choyce but to remayne & behold ranke forgotte,&
ẙ high holde conuerſe wʰ ẙ low as uppon equal
termes, a grete ſcandal did ẙ world heare therof.
    In ẙ heat of ẙ talke it befel ẙ one did breake

wind, yielding an exceding mighty & diftrefsfull stink, whereat all did laffe full fore, and thẽ :

Ye Queene. Verily in mine eight and fixty yeeres have I not heard ẙ fellow to this fart. Me-seemeth, by ẙ grete sound and clamour of it, it was male ; yet ẙ belly it did lurk behinde fhoulde now fall lene & flat agaynft ẙ fpine of him ẙ hath beene delivered of fo ftately & fo vafte a bulke, whereas ẙ guts of them ẙ doe quiff-fplitters bear, ftand comely ftill & rounde. Prithee, lette ẙ author confeffe ẙ offfpring. Wil my Lady Alice teftify ?

Lady Alice. Good your grace, an' I hadde room for such a thunderguft within mine auncient bow-els, 'tis not in reafon I coulde difcharge ẙ same & live to thanck God for ẙ Hee did chufe handmayd so humble whereby to shew his power. Nay, 'tis not I ẙ have broughte forth yˢ ryche o'ermaftering fog, yˢ fragrant gloom, so pray you feeke ye further.

Ye Queene. Mayhap ẙ Lady Margery hath done ẙ companie this favour ?

Lady Margerey. So pleafe you madã, my limbs are feeble wʰ ẙ weighte and drouth of fiue & fixty winters, & it behoveth ẙ I be tender vnto thẽ. In ẙ good providence of God, an' *I* hadde contained yˢ wonder, forfoothe wolde I haue gi'en ẙ whole euening of my finking life to ẙ dribbling of it forth, w^h trembling & vneafy foul,not launched it fuddē in its matchleffe might, takıng myne owne life with uiolence, rending my weak frame like rottē rags. It was not I, your mai^sty.

Ye Queene. O' God's naym, who hath favoured us ? Hath it come to pafs ȳ a fart fhall fart *itfelfe ?* Not foche a one as this, I trow. Young Mafter Beaumont ; but no, 'twould have wafted him to Heav'n like down of goofe's boddy. 'Twas not ȳ little LadyHelen--nay,ne'er blufh,my child; thoul't tickle thy tender maidēhedde with many a moufie-fqueak before thou learneft to blow a harricane like this. Waf't you, my learned & ingenious Jonfon ?

Jonfon. So fell a blaft hath ne'er mine ears saluted,nor yet a ftench fo all-pervading&immortal. 'Twas not a nouice did it,good your maieftie,but one of ueterā experiēce--elfe hadde hee fayled of confidence. In footh it was not I.

Ye Queene. My lord Bacon ?

Lord Bacon. Not from my leāe ētrailes hath this prodigie burft forth,fo pleafe your grace. Nau't doth fo befit ȳ grete as grete performance ;&haply fhall ye finde ȳ 'tis not from mediocrity this miracle hath iffued.

(Tho' ẙ subject bee but a fart, yet will yˢ tedious sink of learning ponderously philosophize. Meantime did ẙ foul&deadly stink peruade all places to ẙ degree, ẙ never smelt I ẙ like, yet dared I not to leave ẙ presēce, albeit I was like to suffocate.)

Ye Queene. What saith ẙ worshipful Master Shaxpur?

Shaxpur. In ẙ grete hãd of God I stand, & so proclaim my innocence. Tho'gh ẙ sinless hosts of Heav'n hadde foretold ẙ comyng of yˢ most desolating breath, proclaiming it a werke of uninspired mã, its quaking thunders, its firmamēt-clogging rottennesse his owne achievemēt in due course of nature, yet hadde not I believed it; but hadde sayd ẙ pit itself hath furnished forth ẙ stink, & Heav'n's artillery hath shook ẙ globe in admiration of it.

(Thē was there a silence, & each did turne him toward ẙ worshipful Sr Walter Ralegh, ẙ brown'd, embatteld, bloudy swashbuckler, who rising vp did smile, & simpering, say :)

Sr. W. Most gracious maiestie, 'twas I ẙ did it, but indeed it was so poor & frail a note, compared with such as I ã wont to furnish, ẙ in sooth I was ashamed to call ẙ weakling mine in soe august a

prefẽce. It was nothing--lefs thã nothing,madam,
I did it but to clere my nether throat ; but hadde
I come prepared thẽ hadde I delivered fomething
worthy.   Bear with mee, pleafe your grace, till I
can make amends.

(Thẽ delivered hee himfelfe of fuch a godleffe &
rocke-fhivering blaft ẙ all were fain to ftop their
ears,& following it did come fo denfe&foul a ftink
ẙ that which went before did feeme a poor&trif-
ling thing befide it.   Thẽ faith he, feigning ẙ he
blufhed&was confufed, *I perceive that I am weak
to-daie & cannot juftice doe vnto my powers ;* &
fat him down as who fholde fay, *There,it is not
moche ; yet he that hath an arse to spare lette
hym fellow that, an' hee think hee can.* ByGod,
an' I were ẙ queene,I wolde e'en tip yˢ fwaggering
braggart out o' the court,& lette him air his gran-
deurs&break his intolerable wynd before ye deaf&
fuch as fuffocation plefeth.)

Thẽ fell they to talke about ẙ manners&cuft'ms
of many peoples,&Mafter Shaxpur fpake of ẙ booke
of ẙ fieur Michael de Montaine,wherein was mention of ẙ couftom of widows of Perigord to wear
vppon ẙ hedde-drefs,in fign of widowhood,a jewel
in ẙ fimilitude of a man's mẽber wilted & limber,

whereat ẙ queene did laffe&say,widows inEngland doe wear prickes too, but 'twixt ẙ thyghs, & not wilted neither,till coition hath done that office for thẽ. Mafter Shaxpur did likewife obferve how ẙ ẙ fieur de Montaine hath alfo fpoken of a certaine emperour of foche mightie proweffe ẙ hee did take ten maidẽ-heddes in ẙ compafs of a fingle night,ẙ while his empreffe did entertain two&twẽty lufty knights atweene her fheetes,yet was not fatiffide ; whereat ẙ merrie Counteffe Granby faith a ram is yet ẙ emperour's fuperiour,fith hee wil tup above an hundred yewes 'twixt funne&funne,&after,if ẙ hee can have none more to fhag, wil mafturbate until hee hath enrych'd whole acres wʰ hys feed.

Thẽ fpake ẙ damned wyndmill,SrWalter, of a people in ẙ vttermoft parts of America ẙ copulate not vntil they be fiue-&-thirty yeeres of age,ẙwomẽ beeing eight-&-twenty,& doe it thẽ but once in fevẽ yeeres.

Ye Queene. How doth thatte like my lyttle LadyHelen ? Shᵃˡˡ wee fend thee thither & preferve thy belly ?

Lady Helen. Pleafe yʳ highneffes grace, mine old nurfe hath told mee there bee more ways of feruing God thã by locking ẙ thyghs together;yet

ã I willing to ſerue him ẙ way too,ſith yovr high-
neſſes grace hath ſet ẙ enſample.

Ye Queene. God's wowndes a goode anſvver,
childe.

Lady Alice. Mayhap 'twill weakẽ whẽ ẙ hair
ſprouts below ẙ navel.

Lady Helen. Nay,it ſprouted two yeeres ſyne;
I can ſcarce more thã cover it with my hãd now.

Ye Queene. Hear ye thatte, my little Beaumonte? Have ye not a ſmalle birde about ye that
ſtirs at hearing tel of ſoe ſweete a neſte?

Beaumonte. 'Tis not inſēſible,illuſtrious madã;
but mouſing owls&bats of low degree may not aſ-
pire to bliſs ſoe whelming & ecſtatic as is found in
ẙ downie neſts of birdes of Paradiſe.

Ye Queene. By ẙ gullet of God, 'tis a neat-
turned complimẽt.   With ſoche a tong as thyne,
lad,thou'lt spread the ivorie thyghs of many a wil-
ing mayd in thy good time, an' thy cod-piece bee
as handy as thy ſpeeche.

Thẽ ſpake ẙ queene of how ſhee met old Rabelais whẽ ſhee was turned of fifteen,& hee did tel
her of a man his father knew that hadde a double
pair of bollocks,whereon a controverſy followed as

concerning the moſt juſt way to ſpell ẏ word, ẏ contention running high 'twixt ẏ learned Bacon & ẏ
ingenious Jonſon, until at laſt ẏ old Lady Margery,
wearying of it all, ſaith, ,,Gentles, what mattereth
it how ye ſhal ſpell ẏ word ? I warrãt ye whẽ ye
use yʳbollocks ye ſhall not think of it;& my Lady
Granby, bee ye content; lette ẏ ſpelling bee; you ſhal
enjoy ẏ beating of them on your buttocks juſt ẏ
ſame, I trow. Before I hadde gained my fourteenth
yeere I hadde learnt ẏ them ẏ would explore a cunt
ſtop'd not to conſider the ſpelling o't.'

Sr W. In ſooth, whẽ a ſhift's turned upp de-
lay is meet for naught but dalliance. Boccaccio
hath a ſtory of a prieſt ẏ did beguile a mayd into
his cell, thẽ knelt him in a corner for to pray for
grace ẏ hee bee rightly thanckfvll for yˢ tẽder maid-
ẽhedde ẏ Lord hadde ſent him; but ẏ abbot ſpying
through ẏ key-hole, did ſee a tuft of browniſh hair
with fair white fleſh about it, wherefore whẽ ẏ
prieſt's prayer was donne, his chance was gone, for-
aſmuch as ẏ lyttle mayd hadde but ẏ one cunt, &
ẏ was already occupied to her content.

Thẽ converſed they of religion, & ẏ mightie
werke ẏ olde dead Luther did doe by ẏ grace of
God. Thẽ next about poetry, & Maſter Shaxpur
did rede a parte of his Kyng Henry iv, ẏ which,

it feemeth vnto mee,is not of ẙ ualve of an arfefvl
of afhes,yet they praifed it bravely,one&all.

Y fame did rede a portion of his ,,Venvs &
Adonis," to their prodigious admiration,vvhereas I,
beeing fleepy & fatigved withal, did deme it but
paltrie ftoffe,& was the more discomforted in ẙ ẙ
bloudie bucanier hadde gotte his wynd again, &
did turne his mind to farting with fuch uillain zeal
ẙ prefently I was like to choke once more. God
damn this wyndy ruffian&all his breed. I wolde ẙ
hell mighte gette hym.

They talked about ẙ wonderful defenfe which
olde Sr Nickolas Throgmorton did make for himfelfe before ẙ judges in ẙ time of Mary; wᶜʰ was
unlvcky matter for to broach, fith it fetched out ẙ
queene with a *Pity yᵗ hee, hauing foe moche wit,
hadde yet not enough to fave his doter's maiden
hedde founde for her marriage-bedde.* And ẙ
queene did give ẙ damn'd Sr.Walter a look ẙ made
hym wince--for fhee hath not forgot hee was her
own lover in ẙ olde daie. There was filent un-
comfortablenefs now ; 'twas not a good turne for
talk to take,fith if ẙ queene muft find offenfe in a
little harmlefse debauching,when pricks were ftiff
& cunts not loath to take ẙ ftiffnefs out of them,
who of yˢ companie was finlefs ; beholde was not

ẙ wife of Maſter Shaxpur four months gone with
child whẽ ſhe ſtood uppe before ẙ altar? Was
not her Grace of Bilgewater roger'd by four lords
before ſhe hadde a huſband? Was not ẙ lyttle
LadyHelen born on her mother's wedding-day?
And, beholde, were not ẙ LadyAlice&ẙ LadyMar-
gery there, mouthing religion, whores from ẙ cra-
dle?

In time came they to diſcourſe of Ceruãtes, &
of ẙ new painter, Rubẽs, ẙ is begynning to bee
heard of. Fine words & dainty-wrought phraſes
from ẙ ladies now, one or two of them beeing, in
other days, pupils of ẙ poor aſs, Lille, himſelf; & I
marked how ẙ Jonſon&Shaxpur did fidget to diſ-
charge ſome uenom of ſarcaſm, yet dared they not
in ẙ preſence, ẙ queene's grace beeing ẙ uery flow-
er of ẙ Euphuiſts herſelfe. But beholde, there bee
they ẙ, having a ſpecialtie, & admiring it in them-
ſelues, bee jealous when a neighbour doth eſſaye it,
nor can bide it in them long. Wherefore 'twas
obſervable ẙ ẙ queene waxed uncontent; &in tyme
a labor'd grandioſe ſpeech out of ẙ mouthe of Lady
Alice, who manifeſtly did mightily pride herſelf
thereon, did quite exhavſte ẙ queene's endurance,
who listened till ẙ gaudy ſpeeche was done, thẽ
lifted up her brows, & with uaſte irony, mincing

fayth, „*Oſhit !*" Whereat they all did laffe, but not ẙ Lady Alice, ẙ olde foolifh bitche.

Now was Sr Walter minded of a tale hee once did hear ẙ ingenious Margrette of Navarre relate, about a maid, which beeing like to fuffer rape by an olde archbifhoppe, did fmartly contriue a deuice to faue her maydẽhedde, &faid to him, „Firft, my lord, I prithee, take out thy holy tool & pifs before mee," wch doing, lo hys member felle, &wolde not rife again.

DONE ATT

Y^e Academie Preffe,

M DCCC LXXX II.

IS SHAKESPEARE DEAD?

IS SHAKESPEARE DEAD ? ? ? ?

MARK TWAIN

WILLIAM SHAKESPEARE

FRANCIS BACON

IS SHAKESPEARE DEAD?

FROM MY AUTOBIOGRAPHY

MARK TWAIN

HARPER & BROTHERS PUBLISHERS
NEW YORK AND LONDON
MCMIX

IS SHAKESPEARE DEAD?

IS SHAKESPEARE DEAD?

FROM MY AUTOBIOGRAPHY

I

SCATTERED here and there through the stacks of unpublished manuscript which constitute this formidable Autobiography and Diary of mine, certain chapters will in some distant future be found which deal with "Claimants" —claimants historically notorious: Satan, Claimant; the Golden Calf, Claimant; the Veiled Prophet of Khorassan, Claimant; Louis XVII., Claimant; William Shakespeare, Claimant; Arthur Orton, Claimant; Mary Baker G. Eddy, Claim-

ant—and the rest of them. Eminent
Claimants, successful Claimants, defeated
Claimants, royal Claimants, pleb Claimants, showy Claimants, shabby Claimants, revered Claimants, despised
Claimants, twinkle starlike here and
there and yonder through the mists of
history and legend and tradition—and
oh, all the darling tribe are clothed in
mystery and romance, and we read about
them with deep interest and discuss them
with loving sympathy or with rancorous
resentment, according to which side we
hitch ourselves to. It has always been
so with the human race. There was never a Claimant that couldn't get a hearing, nor one that couldn't accumulate
a rapturous following, no matter how
flimsy and apparently unauthentic his
claim might be. Arthur Orton's claim
that he was the lost Tichborne baronet
come to life again was as flimsy as Mrs.

Eddy's that she wrote *Science and Health* from the direct dictation of the Deity; yet in England near forty years ago Orton had a huge army of devotees and incorrigible adherents, many of whom remained stubbornly unconvinced after their fat god had been proven an impostor and jailed as a perjurer, and to-day Mrs. Eddy's following is not only immense, but is daily augmenting in numbers and enthusiasm. Orton had many fine and educated minds among his adherents, Mrs. Eddy has had the like among hers from the beginning. Her church is as well equipped in those particulars as is any other church. Claimants can always count upon a following, it doesn't matter who they are, nor what they claim, nor whether they come with documents or without. It was always so. Down out of the long-vanished past, across the abyss of the ages, if you listen you can still hear the believing multitudes shouting for Perkin Warbeck and Lambert Simnel.

A friend has sent me a new book, from England—*The Shakespeare Problem Restated*—well restated and closely reasoned; and my fifty years' interest in that matter—asleep for the last three years—is excited once more. It is an interest which was born of Delia Bacon's book—away back in that ancient day— 1857, or maybe 1856. About a year later my pilot-master, Bixby, transferred me from his own steamboat to the *Pennsylvania*, and placed me under the orders and instructions of George Ealer —dead now, these many, many years. I steered for him a good many months— as was the humble duty of the pilot-apprentice: stood a daylight watch and spun the wheel under the severe superintendence and correction of the master.

4

He was a prime chess player and an idolater of Shakespeare. He would play chess with anybody; even with me, and it cost his official dignity something to do that. Also—quite uninvited—he would read Shakespeare to me; not just casually, but by the hour, when it was his watch, and I was steering. He read well, but not profitably for me, because he constantly injected commands into the text. That broke it all up, mixed it all up, tangled it all up—to that degree, in fact, that if we were in a risky and difficult piece of river an ignorant person couldn't have told, sometimes, which observations were Shakespeare's and which were Ealer's. For instance:

What man dare, *I* dare!
Approach thou *what* are you laying in the leads for? what a hell of an idea! like the rugged ease her off a little, ease her off! rugged Russian bear, the armed rhinoceros

5

or the *there* she goes! meet her, meet her! didn't you *know* she'd smell the reef if you crowded it like that? Hyrcan tiger; take any shape but that and my firm nerves she'll be in the *woods* the first you know! stop the starboard! come ahead strong on the larboard! back the starboard! . . . *Now* then, you're all right; come ahead on the starboard; straighten up and go 'long, never tremble: or be alive again, and dare me to the desert *damnation* can't you keep away from that greasy water? pull her down! snatch her! snatch her baldheaded! with thy sword; if trembling I inhabit then, lay in the leads! —no, only the starboard one, leave the other alone, protest me the baby of a girl. Hence horrible shadow! eight bells—that watchman's asleep again, I reckon, go down and call Brown yourself, unreal mockery, hence!"

He certainly was a good reader, and splendidly thrilling and stormy and tragic, but it was a damage to me, because I have never since been able to read Shakespeare in a calm and sane way.

6

I cannot rid it of his explosive interlardings, they break in everywhere with
their irrelevant "What in hell are you
up to *now!* pull her down! more! *more!*
—there now, steady as you go," and the
other disorganizing interruptions that
were always leaping from his mouth.
When I read Shakespeare now, I can
hear them as plainly as I did in that
long-departed time—fifty-one years ago.
I never regarded Ealer's readings as
educational. Indeed they were a detri-
ment to me.

His contributions to the text seldom
improved it, but barring that detail he
was a good reader, I can say that much
for him. He did not use the book, and
did not need to; he knew his Shakespeare as well as Euclid ever knew his
multiplication table.

Did he have something to say—this
Shakespeare-adoring Mississippi pilot—

anent Delia Bacon's book? Yes. And he said it; said it all the time, for months —in the morning watch, the middle watch, the dog watch; and probably kept it going in his sleep. He bought the literature of the dispute as fast as it appeared, and we discussed it all through thirteen hundred miles of river four times traversed in every thirty-five days—the time required by that swift boat to achieve two round trips. We discussed, and discussed, and discussed, and disputed and disputed and disputed; at any rate *he* did, and I got in a word now and then when he slipped a cog and there was a vacancy. He did his arguing with heat, with energy, with violence; and I did mine with the reserve and moderation of a subordinate who does not like to be flung out of a pilot-house that is perched forty feet above the water. He was fiercely loyal to Shakespeare and cor-

8

dially scornful of Bacon and of all the pretensions of the Baconians. So was I—at first. And at first he was glad that that was my attitude. There were even indications that he admired it; indications dimmed, it is true, by the distance that lay between the lofty boss-pilotical altitude and my lowly one, yet perceptible to me; perceptible, and translatable into a compliment—compliment coming down from above the snow-line and not well thawed in the transit, and not likely to set anything afire, not even a cub-pilot's self-conceit; still a detectable compliment, and precious.

Naturally it flattered me into being more loyal to Shakespeare—if possible— than I was before, and more prejudiced against Bacon—if possible—than I was before. And so we discussed and discussed, both on the same side, and were happy. For a while. Only for a while.

Only for a very little while, a very, very, very little while. Then the atmosphere began to change; began to cool off.

A brighter person would have seen what the trouble was, earlier than I did, perhaps, but I saw it early enough for all practical purposes. You see, he was of an argumentative disposition. Therefore it took him but a little time to get tired of arguing with a person who agreed with everything he said and consequently never furnished him a provocative to flare up and show what he could do when it came to clear, cold, hard, rose - cut, hundred - faceted, diamond-flashing *reasoning*. That was his name for it. It has been applied since, with complacency, as many as several times, in the Bacon-Shakespeare scuffle. On the Shakespeare side.

Then the thing happened which has happened to more persons than to me

when principle and personal interest
found themselves in opposition to each
other and a choice had to be made: I
let principle go, and went over to the
other side. Not the entire way, but far
enough to answer the requirements of
the case. That is to say, I took this
attitude, to wit: I only *believed* Bacon
wrote Shakespeare, whereas I *knew*
Shakespeare didn't. Ealer was satisfied
with that, and the war broke loose.
Study, practice, experience in handling
my end of the matter presently enabled
me to take my new position almost seriously; a little bit later, utterly seriously;
a little later still, lovingly, gratefully,
devotedly; finally: fiercely, rabidly, un-
compromisingly. After that, I was weld-
ed to my faith, I was theoretically ready
to die for it, and I looked down with
compassion not unmixed with scorn,
upon everybody else's faith that didn't

tally with mine. That faith, imposed upon me by self-interest in that ancient day, remains my faith to-day, and in it I find comfort, solace, peace, and never-failing joy. You see how curiously theological it is. The "rice Christian" of the Orient goes through the very same steps, when he is after rice and the missionary is after *him;* he goes for rice, and remains to worship.

Ealer did a lot of our "reasoning"— not to say substantially all of it. The slaves of his cult have a passion for calling it by that large name. We others do not call our inductions and deductions and reductions by any name at all. They show for themselves, what they are, and we can with tranquil confidence leave the world to ennoble them with a title of its own choosing.

Now and then when Ealer had to stop to cough, I pulled my induction-talents together and hove the controversial lead myself: always getting eight feet, eight-and-a-half, often nine, sometimes even quarter-less-twain—as *I* believed; but always "no bottom," as *he* said.

I got the best of him only once. I prepared myself. I wrote out a passage from Shakespeare—it may have been the very one I quoted a while ago, I don't remember—and riddled it with his wild steamboatful interlardings. When an un-risky opportunity offered, one lovely summer day, when we had sounded and buoyed a tangled patch of crossings known as Hell's Half Acre, and were aboard again and he had sneaked the *Pennsylvania* triumphantly through it without once scraping sand, and the *A. T. Lacey* had followed in our wake and got stuck, and he was feeling good, I showed it to him. It amused him. I asked him to fire it off: *read* it; read it,

13

I diplomatically added, as only *he* could read dramatic poetry. The compliment touched him where he lived. He did read it; read it with surpassing fire and spirit; read it as it will never be read again; for *he* knew how to put the right music into those thunderous interlardings and make them seem a part of the text, make them sound as if they were bursting from Shakespeare's own soul, each one of them a golden inspiration and not to be left out without damage to the massed and magnificent whole.

I waited a week, to let the incident fade; waited longer; waited until he brought up for reasonings and vituperation my pet position, my pet argument, the one which I was fondest of, the one which I prized far above all others in my ammunition-wagon, to wit: that Shakespeare couldn't have written Shakespeare's works, for the reason that the man who wrote them was limitlessly familiar with the laws, and the law-courts, and law-proceedings, and lawyer-talk, and lawyer-ways—and if Shakespeare was possessed of the infinitely-divided star - dust that constituted this vast wealth, *how* did he get it, and *where*, and *when?*

"From books."

From books! That was always the idea. I answered as my readings of the champions of my side of the great controversy had taught me to answer: that a man can't handle glibly and easily and comfortably and successfully the *argot* of a trade at which he has not personally served. He will make mistakes; he will not, and cannot, get the trade-phrasings precisely and exactly right; and the moment he departs, by even a shade, from a common trade-form, the reader who has served that trade will know the

writer *hasn't*. Ealer would not be convinced; he said a man could learn how
to correctly handle the subtleties and
mysteries and free-masonries of *any* trade
by careful reading and studying. But
when I got him to read again the passage
from Shakespeare with the interlardings,
he perceived, himself, that books couldn't
teach a student a bewildering multitude
of pilot-phrases so thoroughly and per-
fectly that he could talk them off in
book and play or conversation and make
no mistake that a pilot would not immediately discover. It was a triumph
for me. He was silent awhile, and I
knew what was happening: he was losing
his temper. And I knew he would presently close the session with the same old
argument that was always his stay and
his support in time of need; the same
old argument, the one I couldn't answer
—because I dasn't: the argument that

I was an ass, and better shut up. He delivered it, and I obeyed.

Oh, dear, how long ago it was—how pathetically long ago! And here am I, old, forsaken, forlorn and alone, arranging to get that argument out of somebody again.

When a man has a passion for Shakespeare, it goes without saying that he keeps company with other standard authors. Ealer always had several high-class books in the pilot-house, and he read the same ones over and over again, and did not care to change to newer and fresher ones. He played well on the flute, and greatly enjoyed hearing himself play. So did I. He had a notion that a flute would keep its health better if you took it apart when it was not standing a watch; and so, when it was not on duty it took its rest, disjointed, on the compass-shelf under the breast-board. When the *Pennsylvania* blew up and became a drifting rack-heap freighted with wounded and dying poor souls (my young brother Henry among them), pilot Brown had the watch below, and was probably asleep and never knew what killed him; but Ealer escaped unhurt. He and his pilot-house were shot up into the air; then they fell, and Ealer sank through the ragged cavern where the hurricane deck and the boiler deck had been, and landed in a nest of ruins on the main deck, on top of one of the unexploded boilers, where he lay prone in a fog of scalding and deadly steam. But not for long. He did not lose his head: long familiarity with danger had taught him to keep it, in any and all emergencies. He held his coat-lappels to his nose with one hand, to keep out the steam, and scrabbled around with the other till he found the joints of his flute, then he

18

took measures to save himself alive, and was successful. I was not on board. I had been put ashore in New Orleans by Captain Klinefelter. The reason—however, I have told all about it in the book called *Old Times on the Mississippi*, and it isn't important anyway, it is so long ago.

II

WHEN I was a Sunday-school scholar
something more than sixty years
ago, I became interested in Satan, and
wanted to find out all I could about him.
I began to ask questions, but my class-
teacher, Mr. Barclay the stone-mason,
was reluctant about answering them, it
seemed to me. I was anxious to be
praised for turning my thoughts to serious
subjects when there wasn't another boy
in the village who could be hired to do
such a thing. I was greatly interested
in the incident of Eve and the serpent,
and thought Eve's calmness was per-
fectly noble. I asked Mr. Barclay if he
had ever heard of another woman who,
being approached by a serpent, would

not excuse herself and break for the nearest timber. He did not answer my question, but rebuked me for inquiring into matters above my age and comprehension. I will say for Mr. Barclay that he was willing to tell me the facts of Satan's history, but he stopped there: he wouldn't allow any discussion of them.

In the course of time we exhausted the facts. There were only five or six of them, you could set them all down on a visiting-card. I was disappointed. I had been meditating a biography, and was grieved to find that there were no materials. I said as much, with the tears running down. Mr. Barclay's sympathy and compassion were aroused, for he was a most kind and gentle-spirited man, and he patted me on the head and cheered me up by saying there was a whole vast ocean of materials! I can still feel the happy thrill which these blessed words shot through me.

Then he began to bail out that ocean's riches for my encouragement and joy. Like this: it was "conjectured"— though not established — that Satan was originally an angel in heaven; that he fell; that he rebelled, and brought on a war; that he was defeated, and banished to perdition. Also, "we have reason to believe" that later he did so-and-so; that "we are warranted in supposing" that at a subsequent time he travelled extensively, seeking whom he might devour; that a couple of centuries afterward, "as tradition instructs us," he took up the cruel trade of tempting people to their ruin, with vast and fearful results; that by-and-by, "as the probabilities seem to indicate," he may have done certain things, he might have done certain other things, he must have done still other things.

And so on and so on. We set down the five known facts by themselves, on a piece of paper, and numbered it "page 1"; then on fifteen hundred other pieces of paper we set down the "conjectures," and "suppositions," and "maybes," and "perhapses," and "doubtlesses," and "rumors," and "guesses," and "probabilities," and "likelihoods," and "we are permitted to thinks," and "we are warranted in believings," and "might have beens," and "could have beens," and "must have beens," and "unquestionablys," and "without a shadow of doubts"—and behold!

Materials? Why, we had enough to build a biography of Shakespeare!

Yet he made me put away my pen; he would not let me write the history of Satan. Why? Because, as he said, he had suspicions; suspicions that my attitude in this matter was not reverent;

and that a person must be reverent when writing about the sacred characters. He said any one who spoke flippantly of Satan would be frowned upon by the religious world and also be brought to account.

I assured him, in earnest and sincere words, that he had wholly misconceived my attitude; that I had the highest respect for Satan, and that my reverence for him equalled, and possibly even exceeded, that of any member of any church. I said it wounded me deeply to perceive by his words that he thought I would make fun of Satan, and deride him, laugh at him, scoff at him: whereas in truth I had never thought of such a thing, but had only a warm desire to make fun of those others and laugh at *them.* "What others?" "Why, the Supposers, the Perhapsers, the Might-Have-Beeners, the Could-Have-Beeners, the

Must-Have-Beeners, the Without-a-Shadow-of-Doubters, the We-are-Warranted-in-Believingers, and all that funny crop of solemn architects who have taken a good solid foundation of five indisputable and unimportant facts and built upon it a Conjectural Satan thirty miles high."

What did Mr. Barclay do then? Was he disarmed? Was he silenced? No. He was shocked. He was so shocked that he visibly shuddered. He said the Satanic Traditioners and Perhapsers and Conjecturers were *themselves* sacred! As sacred as their work. So sacred that whoso ventured to mock them or make fun of their work, could not afterward enter any respectable house, even by the back door.

How true were his words, and how wise! How fortunate it would have been for me if I had heeded them. But I was

25

young, I was but seven years of age, and vain, foolish, and anxious to attract attention. I wrote the biography, and have never been in a respectable house since.

III

HOW curious and interesting is the parallel—as far as poverty of biographical details is concerned—between Satan and Shakespeare. It is wonderful, it is unique, it stands quite alone, there is nothing resembling it in history, nothing resembling it in romance, nothing approaching it even in tradition. How sublime is their position, and how overtopping, how sky-reaching, how supreme —the two Great Unknowns, the two Illustrious Conjecturabilities! They are the best-known unknown persons that have ever drawn breath upon the planet.

For the instruction of the ignorant I will make a list, now, of those details of

Shakespeare's history which are *facts*—verified facts, established facts, undisputed facts.

Facts

He was born on the 23d of April, 1564.

Of good farmer-class parents who could not read, could not write, could not sign their names.

At Stratford, a small back settlement which in that day was shabby and unclean, and densely illiterate. Of the nineteen important men charged with the government of the town, thirteen had to "make their mark" in attesting important documents, because they could not write their names.

Of the first eighteen years of his life *nothing* is known. They are a blank.

On the 27th of November (1582) William Shakespeare took out a license to marry Anne Whateley.

Next day William Shakespeare took out a license to marry Anne Hathaway. She was eight years his senior.

William Shakespeare married Anne Hathaway. In a hurry. By grace of a reluctantly-granted dispensation there was but one publication of the banns.

Within six months the first child was born.

About two (blank) years followed, during which period *nothing at all happened to Shakespeare*, so far as anybody knows.

Then came twins—1585. February.

Two blank years follow.

Then—1587—he makes a ten-year visit to London, leaving the family behind.

Five blank years follow. During this period *nothing happened to him*, as far as anybody actually knows.

Then—1592—there is mention of him as an actor.

Next year—1593—his name appears in the official list of players.

Next year—1594—he played before the queen. A detail of no consequence: other obscurities did it every year of the forty-five of her reign. And remained obscure.

Three pretty full years follow. Full of play-acting. Then

In 1597 he bought New Place, Stratford.

Thirteen or fourteen busy years follow; years in which he accumulated money, and also reputation as actor and manager.

Meantime his name, liberally and variously spelt, had become associated with a number of great plays and poems, as (ostensibly) author of the same.

Some of these, in these years and later, were pirated, but he made no protest.

Then—1610–11—he returned to Stratford and settled down for good and all, and busied himself in lending money, trading in tithes, trading in land and houses; shirking a debt of forty-one shillings, borrowed by his wife during his long desertion of his family; suing debtors for shillings and coppers; being sued himself for shillings and coppers; and acting as confederate to a neighbor who tried to rob the town of its rights in a certain common, and did not succeed.

He lived five or six years—till 1616—in the joy of these elevated pursuits. Then he made a will, and signed each of its three pages with his name.

A thoroughgoing business man's will. It named in minute detail every item of property he owned in the world—houses, lands, sword, silver-gilt bowl, and so on —all the way down to his "second-best bed" and its furniture.

It carefully and calculatingly distrib-uted his riches among the members of his family, overlooking no individual of it. Not even his wife: the wife he had been enabled to marry in a hurry by urgent grace of a special dispensation before he was nineteen; the wife whom he had left husbandless so many years; the wife who had had to borrow forty-one shillings in her need, and which the lender was never able to collect of the prosperous husband, but died at last with the money still lacking. No, even this wife was remembered in Shakespeare's will.

He left her that "second-best bed."

And *not another thing;* not even a penny to bless her lucky widowhood with.

It was eminently and conspicuously a business man's will, not a poet's.

It mentioned *not a single book.*

Books were much more precious than swords and silver-gilt bowls and second-best beds in those days, and when a departing person owned one he gave it a high place in his will.

The will mentioned *not a play, not a poem, not an unfinished literary work, not a scrap of manuscript of any kind.*

Many poets have died poor, but this is the only one in history that has died *this* poor; the others all left literary remains behind. Also a book. Maybe two.

If Shakespeare had owned a dog—but we need not go into that: we know he would have mentioned it in his will. If a good dog, Susanna would have got it; if an inferior one his wife would have got a dower interest in it. I wish he had had a dog, just so we could see how painstakingly he would have divided that dog among the family, in his careful business way.

He signed the will in three places.

33

In earlier years he signed two other official documents.

These five signatures still exist.

There are *no other specimens of his penmanship in existence.* Not a line.

Was he prejudiced against the art? His granddaughter, whom he loved, was eight years old when he died, yet she had had no teaching, he left no provision for her education although he was rich, and in her mature womanhood she couldn't write and couldn't tell her husband's manuscript from anybody else's —she thought it was Shakespeare's.

When Shakespeare died in Stratford *it was not an event.* It made no more stir in England than the death of any other forgotten theatre-actor would have made. Nobody came down from London; there were no lamenting poems, no eulogies, no national tears—there was merely silence, and nothing more. A striking

34

contrast with what happened when Ben Jonson, and Francis Bacon, and Spenser, and Raleigh and the other distinguished literary folk of Shakespeare's time passed from life! No praiseful voice was lifted for the lost Bard of Avon; even Ben Jonson waited seven years before he lifted his.

So far as anybody actually knows and can prove, Shakespeare of Stratford-on-Avon never wrote a play in his life.

So far as anybody knows and can prove, he never wrote a letter to anybody in his life.

So far as any one knows, he received only one letter during his life.

So far as any one *knows and can prove*, Shakespeare of Stratford wrote only one poem during his life. This one is authentic. He did write that one—a fact which stands undisputed; he wrote the whole of it; he wrote the whole of it out

35

of his own head. He commanded that this work of art be engraved upon his tomb, and he was obeyed. There it abides to this day. This is it:

> Good friend for Iesus sake forbeare
> To digg the dust encloased heare:
> Blest be ye man yt spares thes stones
> And curst be he yt moves my bones.

In, the list as above set down, will be found *every positively known* fact of Shakespeare's life, lean and meagre as the invoice is. Beyond these details we know *not a thing* about him. All the rest of his vast history, as furnished by the biographers, is built up, course upon course, of guesses, inferences, theories, conjectures—an Eiffel Tower of artificialities rising sky-high from a very flat and very thin foundation of inconsequential facts.

IV

Conjectures

THE historians "suppose" that Shakespeare attended the Free School in
Stratford from the time he was seven
years old till he was thirteen. There is
no *evidence* in existence that he ever
went to school at all.

The historians "infer" that he got his
Latin in that school—the school which
they "suppose" he attended.

They "suppose" his father's declining
fortunes made it necessary for him to
leave the school they supposed he attended, and get to work and help support his parents and their ten children.
But there is no evidence that he ever

entered or retired from the school they suppose he attended.

They "suppose" he assisted his father in the butchering business; and that, being only a boy, he didn't have to do full-grown butchering, but only slaughtered calves. Also, that whenever he killed a calf he made a high-flown speech over it. This supposition rests upon the testimony of a man who wasn't there at the time; a man who got it from a man who could have been there, but did not say whether he was or not; and neither of them thought to mention it for decades, and decades, and decades, and two more decades after Shakespeare's death (until old age and mental decay had refreshed and vivified their memories). They hadn't two facts in stock about the long-dead distinguished citizen, but only just the one: he slaughtered calves and broke into oratory while he

38

was at it. Curious. They had only one fact, yet the distinguished citizen had spent twenty-six years in that little town —just half his lifetime. However, rightly viewed, it was the most important fact, indeed almost the only important fact, of Shakespeare's life in Stratford. Rightly viewed. For experience is an author's most valuable asset; experience is the thing that puts the muscle and the breath and the warm blood into the book he writes. Rightly viewed, calf-butchering accounts for *Titus Andronicus*, the only play—ain't it?—that the Stratford Shakespeare ever wrote; and yet it is the only one everybody tries to chouse him out of, the Baconians included.

The historians find themselves "justified in believing" that the young Shakespeare poached upon Sir Thomas Lucy's deer preserves and got haled before that magistrate for it. But there

39

is no shred of respectworthy evidence
that anything of the kind happened.

The historians, having argued the thing
that *might* have happened into the thing
that *did* happen, found no trouble in
turning Sir Thomas Lucy into Mr. Justice
Shallow. They have long ago convinced
the world—on surmise and without trust-
worthy evidence—that Shallow *is* Sir
Thomas.

The next addition to the young Shakespeare's Stratford history comes easy.
The historian builds it out of the surmised deer-stealing, and the surmised
trial before the magistrate, and the surmised vengeance-prompted satire upon
the magistrate in the play: result, the
young Shakespeare was a wild, wild,
wild, oh *such* a wild young scamp, and
that gratuitous slander is established for
all time! It is the very way Professor
Osborn and I built the colossal skeleton

40

brontosaur that stands fifty-seven feet long and sixteen feet high in the Natural History Museum, the awe and admiration of all the world, the stateliest skeleton that exists on the planet. We had nine bones, and we built the rest of him out of plaster of paris. We ran short of plaster of paris, or we'd have built a brontosaur that could sit down beside the Stratford Shakespeare and none but an expert could tell which was biggest or contained the most plaster.

Shakespeare pronounced *Venus and Adonis* "the first heir of his invention," apparently implying that it was his first effort at literary composition. He should not have said it. It has been an embarrassment to his historians these many, many years. They have to make him write that graceful and polished and flawless and beautiful poem before he escaped from Stratford and his family—

1586 or '87—age, twenty-two, or along there; because within the next five years he wrote five great plays, and could not have found time to write another line.

It is sorely embarrassing. If he began to slaughter calves, and poach deer, and rollick around, and learn English, at the earliest likely moment—say at thirteen, when he was supposably wrenched from that school where he was supposably storing up Latin for future literary use— he had his youthful hands full, and much more than full. He must have had to put aside his Warwickshire dialect, which wouldn't be understood in London, and study English very hard. Very hard indeed; incredibly hard, almost, if the result of that labor was to be the smooth and rounded and flexible and letter-perfect English of the *Venus and Adonis* in the space of ten years; and at the same

time learn great and fine and unsurpass-
able literary *form*.

However, it is "conjectured" that he
accomplished all this and more, much
more: learned law and its intricacies;
and the complex procedure of the law
courts; and all about soldiering, and
sailoring, and the manners and customs
and ways of royal courts and aristocratic
society; and likewise accumulated in
his one head every kind of knowledge
the learned then possessed, and every
kind of humble knowledge possessed by
the lowly and the ignorant; and added
thereto a wider and more intimate
knowledge of the world's great litera-
tures, ancient and modern, than was
possessed by any other man of his time
—for he was going to make brilliant
and easy and admiration - compelling
use of these splendid treasures the
moment he got to London. And accord-

ing to the surmisers, that is what he did. Yes, although there was no one in Stratford able to teach him these things, and no library in the little village to dig them out of. His father could not read, and even the surmisers surmise that he did not keep a library.

It is surmised by the biographers that the young Shakespeare got his vast knowledge of the law and his familiar and accurate acquaintance with the manners and customs and shop-talk of lawyers through being for a time the *clerk of a Stratford court;* just as.a bright lad like me, reared in a village on the banks of the Mississippi, might become perfect in knowledge of the Behring Strait whale-fishery and the shop-talk of the veteran exercisers of that adventure-bristling trade through catching catfish with a "trot-line" Sundays. But the surmise is damaged by the fact that there is no

44

evidence—and not even tradition—that the young Shakespeare was ever clerk of a law court.

It is further surmised that the young Shakespeare accumulated his law-treasures in the first years of his sojourn in London, through "amusing himself" by learning book-law in his garret and by picking up lawyer-talk and the rest of it through loitering about the law-courts and listening. But it is only surmise; there is no *evidence* that he ever did either of those things. They are merely a couple of chunks of plaster of paris.

There is a legend that he got his bread and butter by holding horses in front of the London theatres, mornings and afternoons. Maybe he did. If he did, it seriously shortened his law-study hours and his recreation-time in the courts. In those very days he was writing great plays, and needed all the time he could

45

get. The horse-holding legend ought to be strangled; it too formidably increases the historian's difficulty in accounting for the young Shakespeare's erudition—an erudition which he was acquiring, hunk by hunk and chunk by chunk every day in those strenuous times, and emptying each day's catch into next day's imperishable drama.

He had to acquire a knowledge of war at the same time; and a knowledge of soldier-people and sailor-people and their ways and talk; also a knowledge of some foreign lands and their languages: for he was daily emptying fluent streams of these various knowledges, too, into his dramas. How did he acquire these rich assets?

In the usual way: by surmise. It is *surmised* that he travelled in Italy and Germany and around, and qualified himself to put their scenic and social aspects

46

upon paper; that he perfected himself in French, Italian and Spanish on the road; that he went in Leicester's expedition to the Low Countries, as soldier or sutler or something, for several months or years—or whatever length of time a surmiser needs in his business—and thus became familiar with soldiership and soldier-ways and soldier-talk, and generalship and general-ways and general-talk, and seamanship and sailor-ways and sailor-talk.

Maybe he did all these things, but I would like to know who held the horses in the meantime; and who studied the books in the garret; and who frollicked in the law-courts for recreation. Also, who did the call-boying and the play-acting.

For he became a call-boy; and as early as '93 he became a "vagabond"—the law's ungentle term for an unlisted

47

actor; and in '94 a "regular" and properly and officially listed member of that (in those days) lightly-valued and not much respected profession.

Right soon thereafter he became a stockholder in two theatres, and manager of them. Thenceforward he was a busy and flourishing business man, and was raking in money with both hands for twenty years. Then in a noble frenzy of poetic inspiration he wrote his one poem—his only poem, his darling—and laid him down and died:

Good friend for Iesus sake forbeare
To digg the dust encloased heare:
Blest be ye man yt spares thes stones
And curst be he yt moves my bones.

He was probably dead when he wrote it. Still, this is only conjecture. We have only circumstantial evidence. Internal evidence.

Shall I set down the rest of the Conjectures which constitute the giant Biography of William Shakespeare? It would strain the Unabridged Dictionary to hold them. He is a Brontosaur: nine bones and six hundred barrels of plaster of paris.

V

"We May Assume"

IN the Assuming trade three separate
and independent cults are transacting
business. Two of these cults are known
as the Shakespearites and the Baconians, and I am the other one—the
Brontosaurian.

The Shakespearite knows that Shakespeare wrote Shakespeare's Works; the
Baconian knows that Francis Bacon
wrote them; the Brontosaurian doesn't
really know which of them did it, but
is quite composedly and contentedly sure
that Shakespeare *didn't*, and strongly
suspects that Bacon *did*. We all have
to do a good deal of assuming, but I am

fairly certain that in every case I can call to mind the Baconian assumers have come out ahead of the Shakespearites. Both parties handle the same materials, but the Baconians seem to me to get much more reasonable and rational and persuasive results out of them than is the case with the Shakespearites. The Shakespearite conducts his assuming upon a definite principle, an unchanging and immutable law—which is: 2 and 8 and 7 and 14, added together, make 165. I believe this to be an error. No matter, you cannot get a habit-sodden Shakespearite to cipher-up his materials upon any other basis. With the Baconian it is different. If you place before him the above figures and set him to adding them up, he will never in any case get more than 45 out of them, and in nine cases out of ten he will get just the proper 31.

Let me try to illustrate the two systems in a simple and homely way calculated to bring the idea within the grasp of the ignorant and unintelligent. We will suppose a case: take a lap-bred, house-fed, uneducated, inexperienced kitten; take a rugged old Tom that's scarred from stem to rudder-post with the memorials of strenuous experience, and is so cultured, so educated, so limitlessly erudite that one may say of him "all cat-knowledge is his province"; also, take a mouse. Lock the three up in a holeless, crackless, exitless prison-cell. Wait half an hour, then open the cell, introduce a Shakespearite and a Baconian, and let them cipher and assume. The mouse is missing: the question to be decided is, where is it? You can guess both verdicts beforehand. One verdict will say the kitten contains the mouse; the other will as certainly say the mouse is in the tomcat.

The Shakespearite will Reason like this—(that is not my word, it is his). He will say the kitten *may have been* attending school when nobody was noticing; therefore *we are warranted in assuming* that it did so; also, it *could have been* training in a court-clerk's office when no one was noticing; since that could have happened, *we are justified in assuming* that it did happen; it *could have studied catology in a garret* when no one was noticing—therefore it *did;* it *could have* attended cat-assizes on the shed-roof nights, for recreation, when no one was noticing, and harvested a knowledge of cat court-forms and cat lawyer-talk in that way: it *could* have done it, therefore without a doubt it *did;* it *could have* gone soldiering with a war-tribe when no one was noticing, and learned soldier-wiles and soldier-ways, and what to do with a mouse when opportunity offers;

53

the plain inference, therefore is, that that is what it *did*. Since all these manifold things *could* have occurred, we have *every right to believe* they did occur. These patiently and painstakingly accumulated vast acquirements and competences needed but one thing more—opportunity—to convert themselves into triumphant action. The opportunity came, we have the result; *beyond shadow of question* the mouse is in the kitten.

It is proper to remark that when we of the three cults plant a *"We think we may assume,"* we expect it, under careful watering and fertilizing and tending, to grow up into a strong and hardy and weather-defying *"there isn't a shadow of a doubt"* at last—and it usually happens.

We know what the Baconian's verdict would be: *"There is not a rag of evidence that the kitten has had any training, any education, any experience qualifying it for*

54

the present occasion, or is indeed equipped for any achievement above lifting such un-claimed milk as comes its way; but there is abundant evidence—unassailable proof, in fact—that the other animal is epuipped, to the last detail, with every qualification necessary for the event. Without shadow of doubt the tomcat contains the mouse."

VI

WHEN Shakespeare died, in 1616,
great literary productions attributed to him as author had been before
the London world and in high favor for
twenty-four years. Yet his death was
not an event. It made no stir, it attracted no attention. Apparently his
eminent literary contemporaries did not
realize that a celebrated poet had passed
from their midst. Perhaps they knew a
play-actor of minor rank had disappeared,
but did not regard him as the author of
his Works. "We are justified in assuming" this.

His death was not even an event in the
little town of Stratford. Does this mean

that in Stratford he was not regarded as a celebrity of *any* kind?

"We are privileged to assume"—no, we are indeed *obliged* to assume—that such was the case. He had spent the first twenty-two or twenty-three years of his life there, and of course knew everybody and was known by everybody of that day in the town, including the dogs and the cats and the horses. He had spent the last five or six years of his life there, diligently trading in every big and little thing that had money in it; so we are compelled to assume that many of the folk there in those said latter days knew him personally, and the rest by sight and hearsay. But not as a *celebrity?* Apparently not. For everybody soon forgot to remember any contact with him or any incident connected with him. The dozens of townspeople, still alive, who had known of him or known

57

about him in the first twenty-three years of his life were in the same unremembering condition: if they knew of any incident connected with that period of his life they didn't tell about it. Would they if they had been asked? It is most likely. Were they asked? It is pretty apparent that they were not. Why weren't they? It is a very plausible guess that nobody there or elsewhere was interested to know.

For seven years after Shakespeare's death nobody seems to have been interested in him. Then the quarto was published, and Ben Jonson awoke out of his long indifference and sang a song of praise and put it in the front of the book. Then silence fell *again*.

For sixty years. Then inquiries into Shakespeare's Stratford life began to be made, of Stratfordians. Of Stratfordians who had known Shakespeare or had seen him? No. Then of Stratfordians who had seen people who had known or seen people who had seen Shakespeare? No. Apparently the inquiries were only made of Stratfordians who were not Stratfordians of Shakespeare's day, but later comers; and what they had learned had come to them from persons who had not seen Shakespeare; and what they had learned was not claimed as *fact*, but only as legend—dim and fading and indefinite legend; legend of the calf-slaughtering rank, and not worth remembering either as history or fiction.

Has it ever happened before—or since —that a celebrated person who had spent exactly half of a fairly long life in the village where he was born and reared, was able to slip out of this world and leave that village voiceless and gossipless behind him—utterly voiceless, utterly gossipless? And permanently so?

I don't believe it has happened in any case except Shakespeare's. And couldn't and wouldn't have happened in his case if he had been regarded as a celebrity at the time of his death.

When I examine my own case—but let us do that, and see if it will not be recognizable as exhibiting a condition of things quite likely to result, most likely to result, indeed substantially *sure* to result in the case of a celebrated person, a benefactor of the human race. Like me.

My parents brought me to the village of Hannibal, Missouri, on the banks of the Mississippi, when I was two and a half years old. I entered school at five years of age, and drifted from one school to another in the village during nine and a half years. Then my father died, leaving his family in exceedingly straitened circumstances; wherefore my book-education came to a standstill forever, and I became a printer's apprentice, on board and clothes, and when the clothes failed I got a hymn-book in place of them. This for summer wear, probably. I lived in Hannibal fifteen and a half years, altogether, then ran away, according to the custom of persons who are intending to become celebrated. I never lived there afterward. Four years later I became a "cub" on a Mississippi steamboat in the St. Louis and New Orleans trade, and after a year and a half of hard study and hard work the U. S. inspectors rigorously examined me through a couple of long sittings and decided that I knew every inch of the Mississippi—thirteen hundred miles—in the dark and in the day—as well as a baby knows the way to its mother's paps day or night. So they licensed me as a pilot—knighted me, so to speak— and I rose up clothed with authority, a responsible servant of the United States government.

Now then. Shakespeare died young —he was only fifty-two. He had lived in his native village twenty-six years, or about that. He died celebrated (if you believe everything you read in the books). Yet when he died nobody there or elsewhere took any notice of it; and for sixty years afterward no townsman remembered to say anything about him or about his life in Stratford. When the inquirer came at last he got but one fact —no, *legend*—and got that one at second hand, from a person who had only heard it as a rumor, and didn't claim copyright in it as a production of his own. He couldn't, very well, for its date antedated his own birth-date. But necessarily a number of persons were still alive in Stratford who, in the days of their youth, had seen Shakespeare nearly

62

every day in the last five years of his life, and they would have been able to tell that inquirer some first-hand things about him if he had in those last days been a celebrity and therefore a person of interest to the villagers. Why did not the inquirer hunt them up and interview them? Wasn't it worth while? Wasn't the matter of sufficient consequence? Had the inquirer an engagement to see a dog-fight and couldn't spare the time?

It all seems to mean that he never had any literary celebrity, there or elsewhere, and no considerable repute as actor and manager.

Now then, I am away along in life— my seventy-third year being already well behind me—yet *sixteen* of my Hannibal schoolmates are still alive to-day, and can tell—and do tell—inquirers dozens and dozens of incidents of their

63

young lives and mine together; things
that happened to us in the morning of
life, in the blossom of our youth, in the
good days, the dear days, "the days
when we went gipsying, a long time ago."
Most of them creditable to me, too. One
child to whom I paid court when she was
five years old and I eight still lives in
Hannibal, and she visited me last summer, traversing the necessary ten or
twelve hundred miles of railroad without
damage to her patience or to her old-
young vigor. Another little lassie to
whom I paid attention in Hannibal
when she was nine years old and I the
same, is still alive—in London—and hale
and hearty, just as I am. And on the
few surviving steamboats—those linger-
ing ghosts and remembrancers of great
fleets that plied the big river in the
beginning of my water-career—which is
exactly as long ago as the whole invoice

64

of the life-years of Shakespeare number —there are still findable two or three river-pilots who saw me do creditable things in those ancient days; and several white-headed engineers; and several roustabouts and mates; and several deck-hands who used to heave the lead for me and send up on the still night air the "six — feet — *scant!*" that made me shudder, and the "M-a-r-k—*twain!*" that took the shudder away, and presently the darling "By the d-e-e-p—*four!*" that lifted me to heaven for joy.[1] They know about me, and can tell. And so do printers, from St. Louis to New York; and so do newspaper reporters, from Nevada to San Francisco. And so do the police. If Shakespeare had really been celebrated, like me, Stratford could have told things about him; and if my experience goes for anything, they'd have done it.

[1] Four fathoms—twenty-four feet.

VII

IF I had under my superintendence
a controversy appointed to decide
whether Shakespeare wrote Shakespeare
or not, I believe I would place before
the debaters only the one question, *Was
Shakespeare ever a practicing lawyer?* and
leave everything else out.

It is maintained that the man who
wrote the plays was not merely myriad-
minded, but also myriad-accomplished:
that he not only knew some thousands
of things about human life in all its
shades and grades, and about the hundred arts and trades and crafts and pro-
fessions which men busy themselves in,
but that he could *talk* about the men
and their grades and trades accurately,

making no mistakes. Maybe it is so, but have the experts spoken, or is it only Tom, Dick, and Harry? Does the exhibit stand upon wide, and loose, and eloquent generalizing—which is not evidence, and not proof—or upon details, particulars, statistics, illustrations, demonstrations?

Experts of unchallengeable authority have testified definitely as to only one of Shakespeare's multifarious craft-equipments, so far as my recollections of Shakespeare-Bacon talk abide with me—his law-equipment. I do not remember that Wellington or Napoleon ever examined Shakespeare's battles and sieges and strategies, and then decided and established for good and all, that they were militarily flawless; I do not remember that any Nelson, or Drake or Cook ever examined his seamanship and said it showed profound and accurate

familiarity with that art; I don't remember that any king or prince or duke
has ever testified that Shakespeare was
letter-perfect in his handling of royal
court-manners and the talk and manners
of aristocracies; I don't remember that
any illustrious Latinist or Grecian or
Frenchman or Spaniard or Italian has
proclaimed him a past-master in those
languages; I don't remember—well, I
don't remember that there is *testimony*
—great testimony—imposing testimony
—unanswerable and unattackable testimony as to any of Shakespeare's hundred specialties, except one—the law.

Other things change, with time, and
the student cannot trace back with cer-
tainty the changes that various trades
and their processes and technicalities
have undergone in the long stretch of a
century or two and find out what their
processes and technicalities were in those

early days, but with the law it is different: it is mile-stoned and documented all the way back, and the master of that wonderful trade, that complex and intricate trade, that awe-compelling trade, has competent ways of knowing whether Shakespeare-law is good law or not; and whether his law-court procedure is correct or not, and whether his legal shop-talk is the shop-talk of a veteran practitioner or only a machine-made counterfeit of it gathered from books and from occasional loiterings in Westminster.

Richard H. Dana served two years before the mast, and had every experience that falls to the lot of the sailor before the mast of our day. His sailor-talk flows from his pen with the sure touch and the ease and confidence of a person who has *lived* what he is talking about, not gathered it from books and random listenings. Hear him:

Having hove short, cast off the gaskets, and made the bunt of each sail fast by the jigger, with a man on each yard, at the word the whole canvas of the ship was loosed, and with the greatest rapidity possible everything was sheeted home and hoisted up, the anchor tripped and cat-headed, and the ship under headway.

Again:

The royal yards were all crossed at once, and royals and sky-sails set, and, as we had the wind free, the booms were run out, and all were aloft, active as cats, laying out on the yards and booms, reeving the studding-sail gear; and sail after sail the captain piled upon her, until she was covered with canvas, her sails looking like a great white cloud resting upon a black speck.

Once more. A race in the Pacific:

Our antagonist was in her best trim. Being clear of the point, the breeze became stiff, and the royal-masts bent under our sails, but we would not take them in until we saw three boys spring into the rigging of the *California;* then they were all furled at once, but with orders to our boys to stay aloft at the top-gallant mast-heads and loose them again at the word. It was my duty to furl the fore-royal; and while standing by to loose it again, I had a fine view of the scene. From where I stood, the two vessels seemed nothing but spars and sails, while their narrow decks, far below, slanting over by the force of the wind aloft, appeared hardly capable of supporting the great fabrics raised upon them. The *California* was to windward of us, and had every advantage; yet, while the breeze was stiff we held our own. As soon as it began to slacken she ranged a little ahead, and the order was given to loose the royals. In an instant the gaskets were off and the bunt dropped. "Sheet home the fore-royal!" — "Weather sheet's home!"—"Lee sheet's home!"— "Hoist away, sir!" is bawled from aloft. "Overhaul your clewlines!" shouts the mate. "Aye-aye, sir, all clear!"—"Taut leech!

71

belay! Well the lee brace; haul taut to windward!" and the royals are set.

What would the captain of any sailing-vessel of our time say to that? He would say, "The man that wrote that didn't learn his trade out of a book, he has *been* there!" But would this same captain be competent to sit in judgment upon Shakespeare's seamanship—considering the changes in ships and ship-talk that have necessarily taken place, unrecorded, unremembered, and lost to history in the last three hundred years? It is my conviction that Shakespeare's sailor-talk would be Choctaw to him. For instance —from *The Tempest :*

Master. Boatswain!
Boatswain. Here, master; what cheer?
Master. Good, speak to the mariners: fall to't, yarely, or we run ourselves to ground; bestir, bestir!

72

(*Enter mariners.*)

Boatswain. Heigh, my hearts! cheerly, cheerly, my hearts! yare, yare! Take in the topsail. Tend to the master's whistle. . . . Down with the topmast! yare! lower, lower! Bring her to try wi' the main course. . . . Lay her a-hold, a-hold! Set her two courses. Off to sea again; lay her off.

That will do, for the present; let us yare a little, now, for a change.

If a man should write a book and in it make one of his characters say, "Here, devil, empty the quoins into the standing galley and the imposing stone into the hell-box; assemble the comps around the frisket and let them jeff for takes and be quick about it," I should recognize a mistake or two in the phrasing, and would know that the writer was only a printer theoretically, not practically.

I have been a quartz miner in the silver regions—a pretty hard life; I know all

73

the palaver of that business: I know all about discovery claims and the subordinate claims; I know all about lodes, ledges, outcroppings, dips, spurs, angles, shafts, drifts, inclines, levels, tunnels, air-shafts, "horses," clay casings, granite casings; quartz mills and their batteries; arastras, and how to charge them with quicksilver and sulphate of copper; and how to clean them up, and how to reduce the resulting amalgam in the retorts, and how to cast the bullion into pigs; and finally I know how to screen tailings, and also how to hunt for something less robust to do, and find it. I know the *argot* of the quartz-mining and milling industry familiarly; and so whenever Bret Harte introduces that industry into a story, the first time one of his miners opens his mouth I recognize from his phrasing that Harte got the phrasing by listening—like Shakespeare—I mean

74

the Stratford one—not by experience. No one can talk the quartz dialect correctly without learning it with pick and shovel and drill and fuse.

I have been a surface-miner—gold—and I know all its mysteries, and the dialect that belongs with them; and whenever Harte introduces that industry into a story I know by the phrasing of his characters that neither he nor they have ever served that trade.

I have been a "pocket" miner—a sort of gold mining not findable in any but one little spot in the world, so far as I know. I know how, with horn and water, to find the trail of a pocket and trace it step by step and stage by stage up the mountain to its source, and find the compact little nest of yellow metal reposing in its secret home under the ground. I know the language of that trade, that capricious trade, that fascinating buried-treasure trade, and can catch any writer who tries to use it without having learned it by the sweat of his brow and the labor of his hands.

I know several other trades and the *argot* that goes with them; and whenever a person tries to talk the talk peculiar to any of them without having learned it at its source I can trap him always before he gets far on his road.

And so, as I have already remarked, if I were required to superintend a Bacon-Shakespeare controversy, I would narrow the matter down to a single question— the only one, so far as the previous controversies have informed me, concerning which illustrious experts of unimpeachable competency have testified: *Was the author of Shakespeare's Works a lawyer?* —a lawyer deeply read and of limitless experience? I would put aside the

76

guesses, and surmises, and perhapses, and might-have-beens, and could-have beens, and must-have-beens, and we-are justified-in-presumings, and the rest of those vague spectres and shadows and indefinitenesses, and stand or fall, win or lose, by the verdict rendered by the jury upon that single question. If the verdict was Yes, I should feel quite convinced that the Stratford Shakespeare, the actor, manager, and trader who died so obscure, so forgotten, so destitute of even village consequence that sixty years afterward no fellow-citizen and friend of his later days remembered to tell anything about him, did not write the Works.

Chapter XIII of *The Shakespeare Problem Restated* bears the heading "Shakespeare as a Lawyer," and comprises some fifty pages of expert testimony, with comments thereon, and I

will copy the first nine, as being sufficient
all by themselves, as it seems to me, to
settle the question which I have con-
ceived to be the master-key to the
Shakespeare-Bacon puzzle.

VIII

Shakespeare as a Lawyer [1]

THE Plays and Poems of Shakespeare supply ample evidence that their author not only had a very extensive and accurate knowledge of law, but that he was well acquainted with the manners and customs of members of the Inns of Court and with legal life generally.

"While novelists and dramatists are constantly making mistakes as to the laws of marriage, of wills, and inheritance, to Shakespeare's law, lavishly as he expounds it, there can neither be demurrer, nor bill of exceptions, nor writ of error." Such was the testimony borne by one of the most distinguished lawyers of the nineteenth cen-

[1] From Chapter XIII of " The Shakespeare Problem Restated."

79

tury who was raised to the high office of Lord Chief Justice in 1850, and subsequently became Lord Chancellor. Its weight will, doubtless, be more appreciated by lawyers than by laymen, for only lawyers know how impossible it is for those who have not served an apprenticeship to the law to avoid displaying their ignorance if they venture to employ legal terms and to discuss legal doctrines. "There is nothing so dangerous," wrote Lord Campbell, "as for one not of the craft to tamper with our freemasonry." A layman is certain to betray himself by using some expression which a lawyer would never employ. Mr. Sidney Lee himself supplies us with an example of this. He writes (p. 164): "On February 15, 1609, Shakespeare . . . obtained judgment from a jury against Addenbroke for the payment of No. 6, and No. 1. 5s. 0d. costs." Now a lawyer would never have spoken of obtaining "judgment from a jury," for it is the function of a jury not to deliver judgment (which is the prerogative of the court), but to find a verdict on the facts. The error is, indeed, a venial one, but it is just one of those little things which at once enable a lawyer to know if the writer is a layman or "one of the craft."

But when a layman ventures to plunge deeply into legal subjects, he is naturally apt to make an exhibition of his incompetence. "Let a non-professional man, however acute," writes Lord Campbell again, "presume to talk law, or to draw illustrations from legal science in discussing other subjects, and he will speedily fall into laughable absurdity."

And what does the same high authority say about Shakespeare? He had "a deep technical knowledge of the law," and an easy familiarity with "some of the most abstruse proceedings in English jurisprudence." And again: "Whenever he indulges this propensity he uniformly lays down good law." Of *Henry IV.*, Part 2, he says: "If Lord Eldon could be supposed to have written the play, I do not see how he could be chargeable with having forgotten any of his law while writing it." Charles and Mary Cowden Clarke speak of "the marvelous intimacy which he displays with legal terms, his frequent adoption of them in illustration, and his curiously technical knowledge of their form and force." Malone, himself a lawyer, wrote: "His knowledge of legal terms is not merely such as might be acquired by the casual observation of even his all-comprehending mind; it has the appearance of technical skill." Another lawyer and well-known Shakespearean, Richard Grant White, says: "No dramatist of the time, not even Beaumont, who was the younger son of a judge of the Common Pleas, and who after studying in the Inns of Court abandoned law for the drama, used legal phrases with Shakespeare's readiness and exactness. And the significance of this fact is heightened by another, that it is only to the language of the law that he exhibits this inclination. The phrases peculiar to other occupations serve him on rare occasions by way of description, comparison or illustration, generally when something in the scene suggests them, but legal phrases flow from his pen as part of his vocabulary, and parcel of his thought. Take the word 'purchase' for instance, which, in ordinary use, means to acquire by giving value, but applies in law to all legal modes of obtaining property except by inheritance or descent, and in this peculiar sense the word occurs five times in Shakespeare's thirty-four plays, and only in one single instance in the fifty-four plays of Beaumont and Fletcher. It has been suggested that it was in attendance upon the courts in London that he picked up his legal vocabulary. But this supposition not only fails to account for Shakespeare's peculiar freedom and exactness in the use of that phraseology, it does not even place him in the way of learning those terms his use of which is most remarkable, which are not such as he would have heard at ordinary proceedings at *nisi prius*, but such as refer to the tenure or transfer of real property, 'fine and recovery,' 'statutes merchant,' 'purchase,' 'indenture,' 'tenure,' 'double voucher,' 'fee simple,' 'fee farm,' 'remainder,' 'reversion,' 'forfeiture,' etc. This conveyancer's jargon could not have been picked up by hanging round the courts of law in London two hundred and fifty years ago, when suits as to the title of real property were comparatively rare. And beside, Shakespeare uses his law just as freely in his first plays, written in his first London years, as in those produced at a later period. Just as exactly, too; for the correctness and propriety with which these terms are introduced have compelled the admiration of a Chief Justice and a Lord Chancellor."

Senator Davis wrote: "We seem to have something more than a sciolist's temerity of indulgence in the terms of an unfamiliar art. No legal solecisms will be found. The abstrusest elements of the common law are impressed into a disciplined service. Over and over again, where such knowledge is unexampled in writers unlearned in the law, Shakespeare appears in perfect possession of it. In the law of real property, its rules of tenure and descents, its entails, its fines and recoveries, their vouchers and double vouchers, in the procedure of the Courts, the method of bringing writs and arrests, the nature of actions, the rules of pleading, the law of escapes and of contempt of court, in the principles of evidence, both technical and philosophical, in the distinction between the temporal and spiritual tribunals, in the law of attainder and forfeiture, in the requisites of a valid marriage, in the presumption of legitimacy, in the learning of the law of prerogative, in the inalienable character of the Crown, this mastership appears with surprising authority."

To all this testimony (and there is much more which I have not cited) may now be added that of a great lawyer of our own times, *viz.:* Sir James Plaisted Wilde, Q.C. 1855, created a Baron of the Exchequer in 1860, promoted to the post of Judge-Ordinary and Judge of the Courts of Probate and Divorce in 1863, and better known to the world as Lord Penzance, to which dignity he was raised in 1869. Lord Penzance, as all lawyers know, and as the late Mr. Inderwick, K.C., has testified, was one of the first legal authorities of his day, famous for his "remarkable grasp of legal principles," and "endowed by nature with a remarkable

facility for marshalling facts, and for a clear
expression of his views."

Lord Penzance speaks of Shakespeare's
"perfect familiarity with not only the principles, axioms, and maxims, but the technicalities of English law, a knowledge so
perfect and intimate that he was never in-
correct and never at fault. . . . The mode in
which this knowledge was pressed into service
on all occasions to express his meaning and
illustrate his thoughts, was quite unexampled. He seems to have had a special
pleasure in his complete and ready mastership of it in all its branches. As manifested
in the plays, this legal knowledge and learning had therefore a special character which
places it on a wholly different footing from
the rest of the multifarious knowledge which
is exhibited in page after page of the plays.
At every turn and point at which the author
required a metaphor, simile, or illustration,
his mind ever turned *first* to the law. He
seems almost to have *thought* in legal phrases,
the commonest of legal expressions were
ever at the end of his pen in description or

86

illustration. That he should have descanted in lawyer language when he had a forensic subject in hand, such as Shylock's bond, was to be expected, but the knowledge of law in 'Shakespeare' was exhibited in a far different manner: it protruded itself on all occasions, appropriate or inappropriate, and mingled itself with strains of thought widely divergent from forensic subjects." Again: "To acquire a perfect familiarity with legal principles, and an accurate and ready use of the technical terms and phrases not only of the conveyancer's office but of the pleader's chambers and the Courts at Westminster, nothing short of employment in some career involving constant contact with legal questions and general legal work would be requisite. But a continuous employment involves the element of time, and time was just what the manager of two theatres had not at his disposal. In what portion of Shakespeare's (*i.e.* Shakspere's) career would it be possible to point out that time could be found for the interposition of a legal employment in the chambers or offices of practising lawyers?"

87

Stratfordians, as is well known, casting about for some possible explanation of Shakespeare's extraordinary knowledge of law, have made the suggestion that Shakespeare might, conceivably, have been a clerk in an attorney's office before he came to London. Mr. Collier wrote to Lord Campbell to ask his opinion as to the probability of this being true. His answer was as follows: "You require us to believe implicitly a fact, of which, if true, positive and irrefragable evidence in his own handwriting might have been forthcoming to establish it. Not having been actually enrolled as an attorney, neither the records of the local court at Stratford nor of the superior Courts at Westminster would present his name as being concerned in any suit as an attorney, but it might reasonably have been expected that there would be deeds or wills witnessed by him still extant, and after a very diligent search none such can be discovered."

Upon this Lord Penzance comments: "It cannot be doubted that Lord Campbell was right in this. No young man could have been at work in an attorney's office without being called upon continually to act as a witness, and in many other ways leaving traces of his work and name." There is not a single fact or incident in all that is known of Shakespeare, even by rumor or tradition, which supports this notion of a clerkship. And after much argument and surmise which has been indulged in on this subject, we may, I think, safely put the notion on one side, for no less an authority than Mr. Grant White says finally that the idea of his having been clerk to an attorney has been "blown to pieces."

It is altogether characteristic of Mr. Churton Collins that he, nevertheless, adopts this exploded myth. "That Shakespeare was in early life employed as a clerk in an attorney's office, may be correct. At Stratford there was by royal charter a Court of Record sitting every fortnight, with six attorneys, beside the town clerk, belonging to it, and it is certainly not straining probability to suppose that the young Shakespeare may have had employment in one of

89

them. There is, it is true, no tradition to
this effect, but such traditions as we have
about Shakespeare's occupation between the
time of leaving school and going to London
are so loose and baseless that no confidence
can be placed in them. It is, to say the
least, more probable that he was in an attorney's office than that he was a butcher
killing calves 'in a high style,' and making
speeches over them."

This is a charming specimen of Stratfordian
argument. There is, as we have seen, a very
old tradition that Shakespeare was a butcher's
apprentice. John Dowdall, who made a tour
in Warwickshire in 1693, testifies to it as
coming from the old clerk who showed him
over the church, and it is unhesitatingly
accepted as true by Mr. Halliwell-Phillipps.
(Vol. I, p. 11, and see Vol. II, p. 71, 72.)
Mr. Sidney Lee sees nothing improbable in
it, and it is supported by Aubrey, who must
have written his account some time before
1680, when his manuscript was completed.
Of the attorney's clerk hypothesis, on the
other hand, there is not the faintest vestige

of a tradition. It has been evolved out of the fertile imaginations of embarrassed Stratfordians, seeking for some explanation of the Stratford rustic's marvellous acquaintance with law and legal terms and legal life. But Mr. Churton Collins has not the least hesitation in throwing over the tradition which has the warrant of antiquity and setting up in its stead this ridiculous invention, for which not only is there no shred of positive evidence, but which, as Lord Campbell and Lord Penzance point out, is really put out of court by the negative evidence, since "no young man could have been at work in an attorney's office without being called upon continually to act as a witness, and in many other ways leaving traces of his work and name." And as Mr. Edwards further points out, since the day when Lord Campbell's book was published (between forty and fifty years ago), "every old deed or will, to say nothing of other legal papers, dated during the period of William Shakespeare's youth, has been scrutinized over half a dozen shires, and not one signature of the young man has been found."

Moreover, if Shakespeare had served as clerk in an attorney's office it is clear that he must have so served for a considerable period in order to have gained (if indeed it is credible that he could have so gained) his remarkable knowledge of law. Can we then for a moment believe that, if this had been so, tradition would have been absolutely silent on the matter? That Dowdall's old clerk, over eighty years of age, should have never heard of it (though he was sure enough about the butcher's apprentice), and that all the other ancient witnesses should be in similar ignorance!

But such are the methods of Stratfordian controversy. Tradition is to be scouted when it is found inconvenient, but cited as irrefragable truth when it suits the case. Shakespeare of Stratford was the author of the *Plays* and *Poems*, but the author of the *Plays* and *Poems* could not have been a butcher's apprentice. Away, therefore, with tradition. But the author of the *Plays* and *Poems must* have had a very large and a very accurate knowledge of the law. Therefore,

Shakespeare of Stratford must have been an attorney's clerk! The method is simplicity itself. By similar reasoning Shakespeare has been made a country schoolmaster, a soldier, a physician, a printer, and a good many other things beside, according to the inclination and the exigencies of the commentator. It would not be in the least surprising to find that he was studying Latin as a schoolmaster and law in an attorney's office at the same time.

However, we must do Mr. Collins the justice of saying that he has fully recognized, what is indeed tolerably obvious, that Shakespeare must have had a sound legal training. "It may, of course, be urged," he writes, "that Shakespeare's knowledge of medicine, and particularly that branch of it which related to morbid psychology, is equally remarkable, and that no one has ever contended that he was a physician. (Here Mr. Collins is wrong; that contention also has been put forward.) It may be urged that his acquaintance with the technicalities of other crafts and callings, notably of marine and

93

military affairs, was also extraordinary, and yet no one has suspected him of being a sailor or a soldier. (Wrong again. Why even Messrs. Garnett and Gosse 'suspect' that he was a soldier!) This may be conceded, but the concession hardly furnishes an analogy. To these and all other subjects he recurs occasionally, and in season, but with reminiscences of the law his memory, as is abundantly clear, was simply saturated. In season and out of season now in manifest, now in recondite application, he presses it into the service of expression and illustration. At least a third of his myriad metaphors are derived from it. It would indeed be difficult to find a single act in any of his dramas, nay, in some of them, a single scene, the diction and imagery of which is not colored by it. Much of his law may have been acquired from three books easily accessible to him, namely Tottell's *Precedents* (1572), Pulton's *Statutes* (1578), and Fraunce's *Lawier's Logike* (1588), works with which he certainly seems to have been familiar; but much of it could only have

94

come from one who had an intimate acquaintance with legal proceedings. We quite
agree with Mr. Castle that Shakespeare's
legal knowledge is not what could have been
picked up in an attorney's office, but could
only have been learned by an actual attendance at the Courts, at a Pleader's Chambers, and on circuit, or by associating inti-
mately with members of the Bench and
Bar."

This is excellent. But what is Mr. Collins'
explanation. "Perhaps the simplest solu-
tion of the problem is to accept the hypothesis that in early life he was in an attorney's
office (!), that he there contracted a love for
the law which never left him, that as a young
man in London, he continued to study or
dabble in it for his amusement, to stroll in
leisure hours into the Courts, and to frequent
the society of lawyers. On no other supposition is it possible to explain the attraction
which the law evidently had for him, and his
minute and undeviating accuracy in a subject where no layman who has indulged in
such copious and ostentatious display of

legal technicalities has ever yet succeeded in keeping himself from tripping."

A lame conclusion. "No other supposition" indeed! Yes, there is another, and a very obvious supposition, namely, that Shakespeare was himself a lawyer, well versed in his trade, versed in all the ways of the courts, and living in close intimacy with judges and members of the Inns of Court.

One is, of course, thankful that Mr. Collins has appreciated the fact that Shakespeare must have had a sound legal training, but I may be forgiven if I do not attach quite so much importance to his pronouncements on this branch of the subject as to those of Malone, Lord Campbell, Judge Holmes, Mr. Castle, K.C., Lord Penzance, Mr. Grant White, and other lawyers, who have expressed their opinion on the matter of Shakespeare's legal acquirements. . . .

Here it may, perhaps, be worth while to quote again from Lord Penzance's book as to the suggestion that Shakespeare had somehow or other managed "to acquire a perfect familiarity with legal principles, and an

96

accurate and ready use of the technical terms and phrases, not only of the conveyancer's office, but of the pleader's chambers and the courts at Westminster." This, as Lord Penzance points out, "would require nothing short of employment in some career involving *constant contact* with legal questions and general legal work." But "in what portion of Shakespeare's career would it be possible to point out that time could be found for the interposition of a legal employment in the chambers or offices of practising lawyers? ... It is beyond doubt that at an early period he was called upon to abandon his attendance at school and assist his father, and was soon after, at the age of sixteen, bound apprentice to a trade. While under the obligation of this bond he could not have pursued any other employment. Then he leaves Stratford and comes to London. He has to provide himself with the means of a livelihood, and this he did in some capacity at the theatre. No one doubts that. The holding of horses is scouted by many, and perhaps with justice, as

97

being unlikely and certainly unproved; but whatever the nature of his employment was at the theatre, there is hardly room for the belief that it could have been other than continuous, for his progress there was so rapid. Ere long he had been taken into the company as an actor, and was soon spoken of as a 'Johannes Factotum.' His rapid accumulation of wealth speaks volumes for the constancy and activity of his services. One fails to see when there could be a break in the current of his life at this period of it, giving room or opportunity for legal or indeed any other employment. 'In 1589,' says Knight, 'we have undeniable evidence that he had not only a casual engagement, was not only a salaried servant, as many players were, but was a shareholder in the company of the Queen's players with other shareholders below him on the list.' This (1589) would be within two years after his arrival in London, which is placed by White and Halliwell-Phillipps about the year 1587. The difficulty in supposing that, starting with a state of ignorance in 1587, when he is supposed to have come to London, he was induced to enter upon a course of most extended study and mental culture, is almost insuperable. Still it was physically possible, provided always that he could have had access to the needful books. But this legal training seems to me to stand on a different footing. It is not only unaccountable and incredible, but it is actually negatived by the known facts of his career." Lord Penzance then refers to the fact that "by 1592 (according to the best authority, Mr. Grant White) several of the plays had been written. *The Comedy of Errors* in 1589, *Love's Labour 's Lost* in 1589, *Two Gentlemen of Verona* in 1589 or 1590, and so forth, and then asks, "with this catalogue of dramatic work on hand . . . was it possible that he could have taken a leading part in the management and conduct of two theatres, and if Mr. Phillipps is to be relied upon, taken his share in the performances of the provincial tours of his company—and at the same time devoted himself to the study of the law in all its branches so efficiently as to make himself complete

99

master of its principles and practice, and saturate his mind with all its most technical terms?"

I have cited this passage from Lord Penzance's book, because it lay before me, and I had already quoted from it on the matter of Shakespeare's legal knowledge; but other writers have still better set forth the insuperable difficulties, as they seem to me, which beset the idea that Shakespeare might have found time in some unknown period of early life, amid multifarious other occupations, for the study of classics, literature and law, to say nothing of languages and a few other matters. Lord Penzance further asks his readers: "Did you ever meet with or hear of an instance in which a young man in this country gave himself up to legal studies and engaged in legal employments, which is the only way of becoming familiar with the technicalities of practice, unless with the view of practicing in that profession? I do not believe that it would be easy, or indeed possible, to produce an instance in which the law has been seriously studied in all its

100

branches, except as a qualification for practice in the legal profession."

This testimony is so strong, so direct, so authoritative; and so uncheapened, unwatered by guesses, and surmises, and maybe-so's, and might-have-beens, and could-have-beens, and must-have-beens, and the rest of that ton of plaster of paris out of which the biographers have built the colossal brontosaur which goes by the Stratford actor's name, that it quite convinces me that the man who wrote Shakespeare's Works knew all about law and lawyers. Also, that that man could not have been the Stratford Shakespeare —and *wasn't*.

Who did write these Works, then?

I wish I knew.

IX

DID Francis Bacon write Shakespeare's Works?

Nobody knows.

We cannot say we *know* a thing when that thing has not been proved. *Know* is too strong a word to use when the evidence is not final and absolutely conclusive. We can infer, if we want to, like those slaves. . . . No, I will not write that word, it is not kind, it is not courteous. The upholders of the Stratford-Shakespeare superstition call *us* the hardest names they can think of, and they keep doing it all the time; very well, if they like to descend to that level, let them do it, but I will not so undignify myself as to follow them. I cannot call them harsh names; the most I can do is to indicate them by terms reflecting my disapproval; and this without malice, without venom.

To resume. What I was about to say, was, those thugs have built their entire superstition upon *inferences*, not upon known and established facts. It is a weak method, and poor, and I am glad to be able to say our side never resorts to it while there is anything else to resort to.

But when we must, we must; and we have now arrived at a place of that sort. . . . Since the Stratford Shakespeare couldn't have written the Works, we infer that somebody did. Who was it, then? This requires some more inferring.

Ordinarily when an unsigned poem sweeps across the continent like a tidal wave, whose roar and boom and thunder are made up of admiration, delight and applause, a dozen obscure people rise up and claim the authorship. Why a dozen, instead of only one or two? One reason is, because there's a dozen that are recognizably competent to do that poem. Do you remember "Beautiful Snow"? Do you remember "Rock Me to Sleep, Mother, Rock Me to Sleep"? Do you remember "Backward, turn backward, O Time, in thy flight! Make me a child again just for to-night"? I remember them very well. Their authorship was claimed by most of the grown-up people who were alive at the time, and every claimant had one plausible argument in his favor, at least: to wit, he could have done the authoring; he was competent.

Have the Works been claimed by a dozen? They haven't. There was good reason. The world knows there was but one man on the planet at the time who was competent—not a dozen, and not two. A long time ago the dwellers in a far country used now and then to find a procession of prodigious footprints stretching across the plain—footprints that were three miles apart, each footprint a third of a mile long and a furlong deep, and with forests and villages mashed to mush in it. Was there any doubt as to who had made that mighty trail? Were there a dozen claimants? Were there two? No—the people knew who it was that had been along there: there was only one Hercules.

There has been only one Shakespeare. There couldn't be two; certainly there couldn't be two at the same time. It takes ages to bring forth a Shakespeare, and some more ages to match him. This one was not matched before his time; nor during his time; and hasn't been matched since. The prospect of matching him in our time is not bright.

The Baconians claim that the Stratford Shakespeare was not qualified to write the Works, and that Francis Bacon was. They claim that Bacon possessed the stupendous equipment—both natural and acquired—for the miracle; and that no other Englishman of his day possessed the like; or, indeed, anything closely approaching it.

Macaulay, in his Essay, has much to say about the splendor and horizonless magnitude of that equipment. Also, he has synopsized Bacon's history: a thing which cannot be done for the Stratford Shakespeare, for he hasn't any history to synopsize. Bacon's history is open to the world, from his boyhood to his death in old age—a history consisting of known facts, displayed in minute and multitudinous detail; *facts*, not guesses and conjectures and might-have-beens.

Whereby it appears that he was born of a race of statesmen, and had a Lord Chancellor for his father, and a mother who was "distinguished both as a linguist and a theologian: she corresponded in Greek with Bishop Jewell, and translated his *Apologia* from the Latin so correctly that neither he nor Archbishop Parker could suggest a single alteration." It is the atmosphere we are reared in that determines how our inclinations and aspirations shall tend. The atmosphere furnished by the parents to the son in this present case was an atmosphere saturated with learning; with thinkings and ponderings upon deep subjects; and with polite culture. It had its natural effect. Shakespeare of Stratford was reared in a house which had no use for books, since its owners, his parents, were without education. This may have had an effect upon the son, but we do not know, because we have no history of him of an informing sort. There were but few books anywhere, in that day, and only the well-to-do and highly educated possessed them, they being almost confined to the dead languages. "All the valuable books then extant in all the vernacular dialects of Europe would hardly have filled a single shelf"—imagine it! The few existing books were in the Latin tongue mainly. "A person who was ignorant of it was shut out from all acquaintance—not merely with Cicero and Virgil, but with the most interesting memoirs, state papers, and pamphlets of his own time"—a literature necessary to the Stratford lad, for his fictitious reputation's sake, since the writer of his Works would begin to use it wholesale and in a most masterly way before the lad was hardly more than out of his teens and into his twenties.

At fifteen Bacon was sent to the university, and he spent three years there. Thence he went to Paris in the train of the English Ambassador, and there he mingled daily with the wise, the cultured, the great, and the aristocracy of fashion, during another three years. A total of six years spent at the sources of knowledge; knowledge both of books and of men. The three spent at the university were coeval with the second and last three spent by the little Stratford lad at Stratford school supposedly, and perhapsedly, and maybe, and by inference —with nothing to infer from. The second three of the Baconian six were "presumably" spent by the Stratford lad as apprentice to a butcher. That is, the thugs presume it—on no evidence of any kind. Which is their way, when they want a historical fact. Fact and presumption are, for business purposes, all the same to them. They know the difference, but they also know how to blink it. They know, too, that while in history-building a fact is better than a presumption, it doesn't take a presumption long to bloom into a fact when *they* have the handling of it. They know by old experience that when they get hold of a presumption-tadpole he is not going to *stay* tadpole in their history-tank; no, they know how to develop him into the giant four-legged bullfrog of *fact*, and make him sit up on his hams, and puff out his chin, and look important and insolent and come-to-stay; and assert his genuine simon-pure authenticity with a thundering bellow that will convince everybody because it is so loud. The thug is aware that loudness convinces sixty persons where reasoning convinces but one. I wouldn't be a thug, not even if—but never mind about that, it has nothing to do with the argument, and it is not noble in spirit besides. If I am better than a thug, is the merit mine? No, it is His. Then to Him be the praise. That is the right spirit.

They "presume" the lad severed his "presumed" connection with the Stratford school to become apprentice to a butcher. They also "presume" that the butcher was his father. They don't know. There is no written record of it, nor any other actual evidence. If it would have helped their case any, they would have apprenticed him to thirty butchers, to fifty butchers, to a wilderness of butchers —all by their patented method "presumption." If it will help their case they will do it yet; and if it will further help it, they will "presume" that all those butchers were his father. And the week after, they will *say* it. Why, it is just like being the past tense of the compound reflexive adverbial incandescent hypodermic irregular accusative Noun of Multitude; which is father to the expression which the grammarians call Verb. It is like a whole ancestry, with only one posterity.

To resume. Next, the young Bacon took up the study of law, and mastered that abstruse science. From that day to the end of his life he was daily in close contact with lawyers and judges; not as a casual onlooker in intervals between holding horses in front of a theatre, but as a practicing lawyer—a great and successful one, a renowned one, a Launcelot of the bar, the most formidable lance in the high brotherhood of the legal Table Round; he lived in the law's atmosphere thenceforth, all his years, and by sheer ability forced his way up its difficult steeps to its supremest summit, the Lord Chancellorship, leaving behind him no fellow craftsman qualified to challenge his divine right to that majestic place.

When we read the praises bestowed by Lord Penzance and the other illustrious experts upon the legal condition and legal aptnesses, brilliances, profundities and felicities so prodigally displayed in the Plays, and try to fit them to the history-less Stratford stage-manager, they sound wild, strange, incredible, ludicrous; but when we put them in the mouth of Bacon they do not sound strange, they seem in their natural and rightful place, they seem at home there. Please turn back and read them again. Attributed to Shakespeare of Stratford they are meaningless, they are inebriate extravagancies —intemperate admirations of the dark side of the moon, so to speak; attributed

113

to Bacon, they are admirations of the golden glories of the moon's front side, the moon at the full—and not intemperate, not overwrought, but sane and right, and justified. "At every turn and point at which the author required a metaphor, simile or illustration, his mind ever turned *first* to the law; he seems almost to have *thought* in legal phrases; the commonest legal phrases, the commonest of legal expressions were ever at the end of his pen." That could happen to no one but a person whose *trade* was the law; it could not happen to a dabbler in it. Veteran mariners fill their conversation with sailor-phrases and draw all their similes from the ship and the sea and the storm, but no mere *passenger* ever does it, be he of Stratford or elsewhere; or could do it with anything resembling accuracy, if he were hardy enough to try. Please read again what Lord Campbell and the other great authorities have said about Bacon when they thought they were saying it about Shakespeare of Stratford.

X

The Rest of the Equipment

THE author of the Plays was equipped, beyond every other man of his time, with wisdom, erudition, imagination, capaciousness of mind, grace and majesty of expression. Every one has said it, no one doubts it. Also, he had humor, humor in rich abundance, and always wanting to break out. We have no evidence of any kind that Shakespeare of Stratford possessed any of these gifts or any of these acquirements. The only lines he ever wrote, so far as we know, are substantially barren of them—barren of all of them.

Good friend for Iesus sake forbeare
To digg the dust encloased heare:
Blest be ye man yt spares thes stones
And curst be he yt moves my bones.

Ben Jonson says of Bacon, as orator:

His language, *where he could spare and pass by a jest*, was nobly censorious. No man ever spoke more neatly, more pressly, more weightily, or suffered less emptiness, less idleness, in what he uttered. No member of his speech but consisted of his (its) own graces. . . . The fear of every man that heard him was lest he should make an end.

From Macaulay:

He continued to distinguish himself in Parliament, particularly by his exertions in favor of one excellent measure on which the King's heart was set—the union of England and Scotland. It was not difficult for such an intellect to discover many irresistible arguments in favor of such a scheme. He conducted the great case of the *Post Nati* in the Exchequer Chamber; and the decision of the judges—a decision the legality of which may be questioned, but the beneficial effect of which must be acknowledged —was in a great measure attributed to his dexterous management.

Again:

While actively engaged in the House
of Commons and in the courts of law, he
still found leisure for letters and philosophy.
The noble treatise on the *Advancement of
Learning*, which at a later period was ex-
panded into the *De Augmentis*, appeared in
1605.

The *Wisdom of the Ancients*, a work
which if it had proceeded from any other
writer would have been considered as a
masterpiece of wit and learning, was printed
in 1609.

In the meantime the *Novum Organum* was
slowly proceeding. Several distinguished
men of learning had been permitted to see
portions of that extraordinary book, and
they spoke with the greatest admiration of
his genius.

Even Sir Thomas Bodley, after perusing
the *Cogitata et Visa*, one of the most precious
of those scattered leaves out of which the
great oracular volume was afterward made
up, acknowledged that "in all proposals and

plots in that book, Bacon showed himself
a master workman"; and that "it could not
be gainsaid but all the treatise over did
abound with choice conceits of the present
state of learning, and with worthy con-
templations of the means to procure it."

In 1612 a new edition of the *Essays* appeared, with additions surpassing the original
collection both in bulk and quality.

Nor did these pursuits distract Bacon's
attention from a work the most arduous, the
most glorious, and the most useful that even
his mighty powers could have achieved,
"the reducing and recompiling," to use his
own phrase, "of the laws of England."

To serve the exacting and laborious
offices of Attorney General and Solicitor
General would have satisfied the appetite
of any other man for hard work, but
Bacon had to add the vast literary in-
dustries just described, to satisfy his.
He was a born worker.

The service which he rendered to letters during the last five years of his life, amid ten thousand distractions and vexations, increase the regret with which we think on the many years which he had wasted, to use the words of Sir Thomas Bodley, "on such study as was not worthy such a student."

He commenced a digest of the laws of England, a History of England under the Princes of the House of Tudor, a body of National History, a Philosophical Romance. He made extensive and valuable additions to his Essays. He published the inestimable *Treatise De Argumentis Scientiarum.*

Did these labors of Hercules fill up his time to his contentment, and quiet his appetite for work? Not entirely:

The trifles with which he amused himself in hours of pain and languor bore the mark of his mind. *The best jestbook in the world* is that which he dictated from memory, without referring to any book, on a day on which illness had rendered him incapable of serious study.

Here are some scattered remarks (from Macaulay) which throw light upon Bacon, and seem to indicate—and maybe demonstrate—that he was competent to write the Plays and Poems:

With great minuteness of observation he had an amplitude of comprehension such as has never yet been vouchsafed to any other human being.

The "Essays" contain abundant proofs that no nice feature of character, no peculiarity in the ordering of a house, a garden or a court-masque, could escape the notice of one whose mind was capable of taking in the whole world of knowledge.

His understanding resembled the tent which the fairy Paribanou gave to Prince Ahmed: fold it, and it seemed a toy for the hand of a lady; spread it, and the armies of powerful Sultans might repose beneath its shade.

The knowledge in which Bacon excelled

all men was a knowledge of the mutual relations of all departments of knowledge.

In a letter written when he was only thirty-
one, to his uncle, Lord Burleigh, he said, " I
have taken all knowledge to be my province."

Though Bacon did not arm his philosophy
with the weapons of logic, he adorned her
profusely with all the richest decorations of
rhetoric.

The practical faculty was powerful in
Bacon; but not, like his wit, so powerful as
occasionally to usurp the place of his reason,
and to tyrannize over the whole man.

There are too many places in the Plays
where this happens. Poor old dying
John of Gaunt volleying second-rate
puns at his own name, is a pathetic
instance of it. "We may assume" that
it is Bacon's fault, but the Stratford
Shakespeare has to bear the blame.

No imagination was ever at once so strong

and so thoroughly subjugated. It stopped at the first check from good sense.

In truth much of Bacon's life was passed in a visionary world—amid things as strange as any that are described in the "Arabian Tales" . . . amid buildings more sumptuous than the palace of Aladdin, fountains more wonderful than the golden water of Parizade, conveyances more rapid than the hippogryph of Ruggiero, arms more formidable than the lance of Astolfo, remedies more efficacious than the balsam of Fierabras. Yet in his magnificent day-dreams there was nothing wild—nothing but what sober reason sanctioned.

Bacon's greatest performance is the first book of the *Novum Organum*. . . . Every part of it blazes with wit, but with wit which is employed only to illustrate and decorate truth. No book ever made so great a revolution in the mode of thinking, overthrew so many prejudices, introduced so many new opinions.

9   123

But what we most admire is the vast capacity of that intellect which, without effort, takes in at once all the domains of science—all the past, the present and the future, all the errors of two thousand years, all the encouraging signs of the passing times, all the bright hopes of the coming age.

He had a wonderful talent for packing thought close and rendering it portable.

His eloquence would alone have entitled him to a high rank in literature.

It is evident that he had each and every one of the mental gifts and each and every one of the acquirements that are so prodigally displayed in the Plays and Poems, and in much higher and richer degree than any other man of his time or of any previous time. He was a genius without a mate, a prodigy not matable. There was only one of him; the planet could not produce two of

124

him at one birth, nor in one age. He could have written anything that is in the Plays and Poems. He could have written this:

The cloud-cap'd towers, the gorgeous palaces,
The solemn temples, the great globe itself,
Yea, all which it inherit, shall dissolve,
And, like an insubstantial pageant faded,
Leave not a rack behind. We are such stuff
As dreams are made on, and our little life
Is rounded with a sleep.

Also, he could have written this, but he refrained:

Good friend for Iesus sake forbeare
To digg the dust encloased heare:
Blest be ye man yt spares thes stones
And curst be ye yt moves my bones.

When a person reads the noble verses about the cloud-cap'd towers, he ought not to follow it immediately with Good friend for Iesus sake forbeare, because he will find the transition from great poetry to poor prose too violent for comfort. It will give him a shock. You never notice how commonplace and unpoetic gravel is, until you bite into a layer of it in a pie.

XI

AM I trying to convince anybody that Shakespeare did not write Shakespeare's Works? Ah, now, what do you take me for? Would I be so soft as that, after having known the human race familiarly for nearly seventy-four years? It would grieve me to know that any one could think so injuriously of me, so uncomplimentarily, so unadmiringly of me. No-no, I am aware that when even the brightest mind in our world has been trained up from childhood in a superstition of any kind, it will never be possible for that mind, in its maturity, to examine sincerely, dispassionately, and conscientiously any evidence or any circumstance which shall seem to cast a

doubt upon the validity of that superstition. I doubt if I could do it myself.
We always get at second hand our notions
about systems of government; and high-
tariff and low-tariff; and prohibition and
anti-prohibition; and the holiness of
peace and the glories of war; and codes
of honor and codes of morals; and ap-
proval of the duel and disapproval of it;
and our beliefs concerning the nature of
cats; and our ideas as to whether the
murder of helpless wild animals is base
or is heroic; and our preferences in the
matter of religious and political parties;
and our acceptance or rejection of the
Shakespeares and the Arthur Ortons and
the Mrs. Eddys. We get them all at
second-hand, we reason none of them
out for ourselves. It is the way we are
made. It is the way we are all made,
and we can't help it, we can't change it.
And whenever we have been furnished

128

a fetish, and have been taught to believe in it, and love it and worship it, and refrain from examining it, there is no evidence, howsoever clear and strong, that can persuade us to withdraw from it our loyalty and our devotion. In morals, conduct, and beliefs we take the color of our environment and associations, and it is a color that can safely be warranted to wash. Whenever we have been furnished with a tar baby ostensibly stuffed with jewels, and warned that it will be dishonorable and irreverent to disembowel it and test the jewels, we keep our sacrilegious hands off it. We submit, not reluctantly, but rather gladly, for we are privately afraid we should find, upon examination, that the jewels are of the sort that are manufactured at North Adams, Mass.

I haven't any idea that Shakespeare will have to vacate his pedestal this side of the year 2209. Disbelief in him cannot come swiftly, disbelief in a healthy and deeply-loved tar baby has never been known to disintegrate swiftly, it is a very slow process. It took several thousand years to convince our fine race—including every splendid intellect in it—that there is no such thing as a witch; it has taken several thousand years to convince that same fine race—including every splendid intellect in it— that there is no such person as Satan; it has taken several centuries to remove perdition from the Protestant Church's program of postmortem entertainments; it has taken a weary long time to persuade American Presbyterians to give up infant damnation and try to bear it the best they can; and it looks as if their Scotch brethren will still be burning babies in the everlasting fires when Shakespeare comes down from his perch.

We are The Reasoning Race. We can't prove it by the above examples, and we can't prove it by the miraculous "histories" built by those Stratfordolaters out of a hatful of rags and a barrel of sawdust, but there is a plenty of other things we can prove it by, if I could think of them. We are The Reasoning Race, and when we find a vague file of chipmunk-tracks stringing through the dust of Stratford village, we know by our reasoning powers that Hercules has been along there. I feel that our fetish is safe for three centuries yet. The bust, too —there in the Stratford Church. The precious bust, the priceless bust, the calm bust, the serene bust, the emotionless bust, with the dandy moustache, and the putty face, unseamed of care— that face which has looked passionlessly down upon the awed pilgrim for a hundred and fifty years and will still

look down upon the awed pilgrim three
hundred more, with the deep, deep, deep,
subtle, subtle, subtle, expression of a
bladder.

XII

Irreverence

ONE of the most trying defects which I find in these—these—what shall I call them? for I will not apply injurious epithets to them, the way they do to us, such violations of courtesy being repugnant to my nature and my dignity. The furthest I can go in that direction is to call them by names of limited reverence—names merely descriptive, never unkind, never offensive, never tainted by harsh feeling. If *they* would do like this, they would feel better in their hearts. Very well, then—to proceed. One of the most trying defects which I find in these Stratfordolaters, these

Shakespero ds, these thugs, these bangalores, these troglodytes, these herumfrodites, these blatherskites, these buccaneers, these bandoleers, is their spirit
of irreverence. It is detectable in every
utterance of theirs when they are talking
about us. I am thankful that in me
there is nothing of that spirit. When a
thing is sacred to me it is impossible for
me to be irreverent toward it. I cannot
call to mind a single instance where I
have ever been irreverent, except toward
the things which were sacred to other
people. Am I in the right? I think so.
But I ask no one to take my unsupported
word; no, look at the dictionary; let the
dictionary decide. Here is the definition:

Irreverence. The quality or condition of
irreverence toward God and sacred things.

What does the Hindu say? He says
it is correct. He says irreverence is lack

of respect for Vishnu, and Brahma, and Chrishna, and his other gods, and for his sacred cattle, and for his temples and the things within them. He endorses the definition, you see; and there are 300,000,-000 Hindus or their equivalents back of him.

The dictionary had the acute idea that by using the capital G it could restrict irreverence to lack of reverence for *our* Deity and our sacred things, but that ingenious and rather sly idea miscarried: for by the simple process of spelling *his* deities with capitals the Hindu confiscates the definition and restricts it to his own sects, thus making it clearly compulsory upon us to revere *his* gods and *his* sacred things, and nobody's else. We can't say a word, for he has our own dictionary at his back, and its decision is final.

This law, reduced to its simplest terms, is this: 1. Whatever is sacred to the

135

Christian must be held in reverence by everybody else; 2, whatever is sacred to the Hindu must be held in reverence by everybody else; 3, therefore, by consequence, logically, and indisputably, whatever is sacred to *me* must be held in reverence by everybody else.

Now then, what aggravates me is, that these troglodytes and muscovites and bandoleers and buccaneers are *also* trying to crowd in and share the benefit of the law, and compel everybody to revere their Shakespeare and hold him sacred. We can't have that: there's enough of us already. If you go on widening and spreading and inflating the privilege, it will presently come to be conceded that each man's sacred things are the *only* ones, and the rest of the human race will have to be humbly reverent toward them or suffer for it. That can surely happen, and when it happens, the word

Irreverence will be regarded as the most meaningless, and foolish, and self-conceited, and insolent, and impudent and dictatorial word in the language. And people will say, "Whose business is it, what gods I worship and what things hold sacred? Who has the right to dictate to my conscience, and where did he get that right?"

We cannot afford to let that calamity come upon us. We must save the word from this destruction. There is but one way to do it, and that is, to stop the spread of the privilege, and strictly confine it to its present limits: that is, to all the Christian sects, to all the Hindu sects, and me. We do not need any more, the stock is watered enough, just as it is.

It would be better if the privilege were limited to me alone. I think so because I am the only sect that knows how to employ it gently, kindly, charitably, dispassionately. The other sects lack the quality of self-restraint. The Catholic Church says the most irreverent things about matters which are sacred to the Protestants, and the Protestant Church retorts in kind about the confessional and other matters which Catholics hold sacred; then both of these irreverencers turn upon Thomas Paine and charge *him* with irreverence. This is all unfortunate, because it makes it difficult for students equipped with only a low grade of mentality to find out what Irreverence really *is*.

It will surely be much better all around if the privilege of regulating the irreverent and keeping them in order shall eventually be withdrawn from all the sects but me. Then there will be no more quarrelling, no more bandying of disrespectful epithets, no more heart burnings.

There will then be nothing sacred involved in this Bacon-Shakespeare controversy except what is sacred to me. That will simplify the whole matter, and trouble will cease. There will be irreverence no longer, because I will not allow it. The first time those criminals charge me with irreverence for calling their Stratford myth an Arthur-Orton-Mary-Baker-Thompson-Eddy-Louis-the-Seventeenth-Veiled-Prophet-of-Khorassan will be the last. Taught by the methods found effective in extinguishing earlier offenders by the Inquisition, of holy memory, I shall know how to quiet them.

10

XIII

ISN'T it odd, when you think of it: that you may list all the celebrated Englishmen, Irishmen, and Scotchmen of modern times, clear back to the first Tudors—a list containing five hundred names, shall we say?—and you can go to the histories, biographies and cyclopedias and learn the particulars of the lives of every one of them. Every one of them except one—the most famous, the most renowned—by far the most illustrious of them all—Shakespeare! You can get the details of the lives of all the celebrated ecclesiastics in the list; all the celebrated tragedians, comedians, singers, dancers, orators, judges, lawyers, poets, dramatists, historians, biographers, editors, inventors, reformers, statesmen, generals, admirals, discoverers, prize-fighters, murderers, pirates, conspirators, horse - jockeys, bunco - steerers, misers, swindlers, explorers, adventurers by land and sea, bankers, financiers, astronomers, naturalists, Claimants, impostors, chemists, biologists, geologists, philologists, college presidents and professors, architects, engineers, painters, sculptors, politicians, agitators, rebels, revolutionists, patriots, demagogues, clowns, cooks, freaks, philosophers, burglars, highwaymen, journalists, physicians, surgeons—you can get the life-histories of all of them but *one*. Just *one*—the most extraordinary and the most celebrated of them all—Shakespeare!

You may add to the list the thousand celebrated persons furnished by the rest of Christendom in the past four centuries, and you can find out the life-histories of all those people, too. You will then have listed 1500 celebrities, and you can trace the authentic life-histories of the whole of them. Save one—far and away the most colossal prodigy of the entire accumulation—Shakespeare! About him you can find out *nothing*. Nothing of even the slightest importance. Nothing worth the trouble of stowing away in your memory. Nothing that even remotely indicates that he was ever anything more than a distinctly commonplace person—a manager, an actor of inferior grade, a small trader in a small village that did not regard him as a person of any consequence, and had forgotten all about him before he was fairly cold in his grave. We can go to the records and find out the life-history of every renowned *race-horse* of modern times—but not Shakespeare's! There are many reasons why, and they have

142

been furnished in cartloads (of guess and conjecture) by those troglodytes; but there is one that is worth all the rest of the reasons put together, and is abundantly sufficient all by itself—*he hadn't any history to record.* There is no way of getting around that deadly fact. And no sane way has yet been discovered of getting around its formidable significance.

Its quite plain significance—to any but those thugs (I do not use the term unkindly) is, that Shakespeare had no prominence while he lived, and none until he had been dead two or three generations. The Plays enjoyed high fame from the beginning; and if he wrote them it seems a pity the world did not find it out. He ought to have explained that he was the author, and not merely a *nom de plume* for another man to hide behind. If he had been less intemperately solicitous about his bones, and more solicitous

143

about his Works, it would have been
better for his good name, and a kindness
to us. The bones were not important.
They will moulder away, they will turn
to dust, but the Works will endure until
the last sun goes down.

MARK TWAIN.

P.S. March 25. About two months
ago I was illuminating this Autobiography
with some notions of mine concerning
the Bacon-Shakespeare controversy, and
I then took occasion to air the opinion
that the Stratford Shakespeare was a
person of no public consequence or celebrity during his lifetime, but was utterly
obscure and unimportant. And not only
in great London, but also in the little
village where he was born, where he
lived a quarter of a century, and where
he died and was buried. I argued that
if he had been a person of any note at

144

all, aged villagers would have had much
to tell about him many and many a year
after his death, instead of being unable
to furnish inquirers a single fact connected with him. I believed, and I still
believe, that if he had been famous, his
notoriety would have lasted as long as
mine has lasted in my native village out
in Missouri. It is a good argument, a
prodigiously strong one, and a most
formidable one for even the most gifted,
and ingenious, and plausible Stratford-
olater to get around or explain away.
To-day a Hannibal *Courier-Post* of recent
date has reached me, with an article in it
which reinforces my contention that a
really celebrated person cannot be forgotten in his village in the short space of
sixty years. I will make an extract from it:

Hannibal, as a city, may have many sins
to answer for, but ingratitude is not one of

them, or reverence for the great men she has produced, and as the years go by her greatest son Mark Twain, or S. L. Clemens as a few of the unlettered call him, grows in the estimation and regard of the residents of the town he made famous and the town that made him famous. His name is associated with every old building that is torn down to make way for the modern structures demanded by a rapidly growing city, and with every hill or cave over or through which he might by any possibility have roamed, while the many points of interest which he wove into his stories, such as Holiday Hill, Jackson's Island, or Mark Twain Cave, are now monuments to his genius. Hannibal is glad of any opportunity to do him honor as he has honored her.

So it has happened that the "old timers" who went to school with Mark or were with him on some of his usual escapades have been honored with large audiences whenever they were in a reminiscent mood and condescended to tell of their intimacy with the ordinary boy who came to be a very extraordinary humorist and whose every boyish act is now seen to have been indicative of what was to come. Like Aunt Beckey and Mrs. Clemens, they can now see that Mark was hardly appreciated when he lived here and that the things he did as a boy and was whipped for doing were not all bad after all. So they have been in no hesitancy about drawing out the bad things he did as well as the good in their efforts to get a "Mark Twain story," all incidents being viewed in the light of his present fame, until the volume of "Twainiana" is already considerable and growing in proportion as the "old timers" drop away and the stories are retold second and third hand by their descendants. With some seventy-three years young and living in a villa instead of a house he is a fair target, and let him incorporate, copyright, or patent himself as he will, there are some of his "works" that will go swooping up Hannibal chimneys as long as gray-beards gather about the fires and begin with "I've heard father tell" or possibly "Once when I."

The Mrs. Clemens referred to is my mother—*was* my mother.

And here is another extract from a Hannibal paper. Of date twenty days ago:

Miss Becca Blankenship died at the home of William Dickason, 408 Rock Street, at 2.30 o'clock yesterday afternoon, aged 72 years. The deceased was a sister of "Huckleberry Finn," one of the famous characters in Mark Twain's *Tom Sawyer*. She had been a member of the Dickason family—the housekeeper—for nearly forty-five years, and was a highly respected lady. For the past eight years she had been an invalid, but was as well cared for by Mr. Dickason and his family as if she had been a near relative. She was a member of the Park Methodist Church and a Christian woman.

I remember her well. I have a picture of her in my mind which was graven there, clear and sharp and vivid, sixty-three years ago, She was at that time nine years old, and I was about eleven. I remember where she stood, and how she looked; and I can still see her bare feet, her bare head, her brown face, and her short tow-linen frock. She was crying. What it was about, I have long ago forgotten. But it was the tears that preserved the picture for me, no doubt. She was a good child, I can say that for her. She knew me nearly seventy years ago. Did she forget me, in the course of time? I think not. If she had lived in Stratford in Shakespeare's time, would she have forgotten him? Yes. For he was never famous during his lifetime, he was utterly obscure in Stratford, and there wouldn't be any occasion to remember him after he had been dead a week.

"Injun Joe," "Jimmy Finn," and "General Gaines" were prominent and very intemperate ne'er-do-weels in Hannibal two generations ago. Plenty of gray-heads there remember them to this day, and can tell you about them. Isn't it curious that two "town-drunkards" and one half-breed loafer should leave behind them, in a remote Missourian village, a fame a hundred times greater and several hundred times more particularized in the matter of definite facts than Shakespeare left behind him in the village where he had lived the half of his lifetime?

MARK TWAIN.

THE END

AFTERWORD
1601 and *Is Shakespeare Dead?*
Leslie A. Fiedler

t has always seemed to me regrettable that many readers of
Mark Twain, including some of his most ardent admirers,
are unaware of the existence of his hard-core pornographic
skit originally entitled *Conversation, As It was by the Social
Fireside, in the Time of the Tudors*, but later called simply *1601*. Twain himself
never kept it a secret — except from his wife and daughters — not did he ever
forget it. Though he wrote it in 1876, at a moment when he had bogged down
in his eight-year-long, off-again-on-again writing of *Adventures of Huckleberry
Finn*, he was still reminiscing about its origins until shortly before his death.
In his autobiography he explains how, preparing to write *The Prince and the
Pauper*, he had been "reading ancient English books with the purpose of
saturating myself with archaic English . . . and . . . had been impressed with
the frank indelicacies of speech permissible among ladies and gentlemen of
that ancient time."

Simultaneously envious of and appalled by the titillating freedom lost
in what he considered his own morally superior but less colorful age, he
determined "to contrive one of those stirring conversations out of my own
head." He chose finally not to report it directly, but as recorded by "a dried up
old nobleman," who bitterly remarks on the speech and manners of Queen
Elizabeth and her courtiers. The pleasure he found in reproducing their

gross conversation, Twain goes on to say, was "as nothing to that which was afforded me by the outraged old cupbearer's comments."

In conclusion, however, Twain confesses that he has not recently reread *1601*; and that he intends, therefore, "to examine that masterpiece and see whether it is really a masterpiece or not." Apparently, he never got around to doing so, but Albert Paine, his official biographer, did, and declared, "*1601* is a genuine classic, as classics of that sort go . . . and perhaps, in some day to come, the taste that justified *Gargantua* and the *Decameron* will give the literary refugee shelter and setting among the conventional writings of Mark Twain."

Alas, this has not come to pass. Despite the much touted "sexual revolutions" of the present century and the disappearance of old verbal taboos, *1601* has continued to lead an underground, semi-respectable life, appearing until now only in sometimes bootlegged and always limited editions. Originally, indeed, it was intended for an audience limited to one; having been sent as a letter to Joseph Twichell, Twain's pastor and lifelong friend. Remote from everyone else, they would read passages from it aloud to each other on their customary weekend walks in the woods, rolling on the fallen leaves and laughing until they were "lame and sore."

Such secret sharing of pornography behind the backs of their womenfolk constituted in Victorian times a ritual of male bonding, like cussing, drinking, smoking cigars and shooting pool. In this case, evidently, it seemed to Twichell too satisfactory a one to be confined to a single pair. Consequently, he sent a copy to a mutual friend, Dean Sage, who in turn dropped it, as if inadvertently, onto the floor of the smoking compartment of a train, then still a male preserve. There it was picked up, passed from hand to hand and so extravagantly praised that Sage felt impelled to make it available to a larger audience. He therefore had "a dozen copies" printed on a press in Brooklyn, and "sent one to David Gray in Buffalo, one to a friend in Japan, one to Lord Houghton in England and one to a Jewish Rabbi in Albany, a learned man . . . and lover of old time literature."

So, at any rate, Twain reported later. But he is notoriously unreliable, as he himself admits elsewhere in the autobiography, warning his readers, "I don't believe the details are right but I don't care a rap. They will do just as well as the facts." In fact, *1601* was not first printed in Brooklyn, but in Cleveland, under the auspices of the Vampire Club, at the behest not of Dean Sage but of John Hay — an older and closer friend of Twain's who later became ambassador to Great Britain and secretary of state under Presidents McKinley and Theodore Roosevelt. Though his own manuscript copy had been worn to rags by much reading and rereading, when another friend called Alexander Gunn proposed setting it up in type and running off a few proofs, Hay at first demurred, protesting, "I cannot properly consent . . . as I am afraid that the great man would think I was taking unfair advantage." He then added, thus betraying how hypocritical his demurral was, ". . . if in spite of my prohibition, you take those proofs, send me one."

How Hay got hold of a manuscript copy to begin with remains unclear. The best guess is that it was passed on to him by William Dean Howells, to whom Twain had sent it earlier, along with a mocking letter purporting to submit his disreputable little essay for publication in the eminently respectable *Atlantic Monthly*, of which Howells was then the editor. "If you do not need this for the contributor's column," Twain wrote, "will you please return it to me, as they want it for the Christian Union." Since Howells left behind no record of his reaction, we can only surmise what it was from the general comments on Twain's bawdry which he allowed to be printed after his friend's death.

"He had," Howells wrote at that point, "the Southwestern, the Lincolnian, the Elizabethan breadth of parlance . . . which I suppose one ought not to call coarse without calling oneself prudish; and I was often hiding away in discreet holes and corners the letters in which he had loosed his bold fancy to stoop on suggestion." In the case of *1601*, however, instead of hiding it away, Howells sent it on to Hay, thus setting in motion the chain of events which led to its first modest publication, after which Twain was almost overwhelmed by a flood of letters: fulsome praise from those lucky enough to have been recipients of the few printed copies, and urgent requests to see one from those who had not.

What seems to have moved him most deeply was a communication from

David Gray, who had been his sole companion and comforter in those terrible fourteen months in Buffalo, following his marriage, when he was plagued by the deaths and illnesses of family and friends. Certainly, Twain never forgot Gray's encouraging missive, actually quoting it word for word twenty-five years later in his autobiography. "Put your name on it," he tells us Gray wrote him. "Don't be ashamed of it. It is a great and fine piece of literature and deserves to live, and will live. Your Innocents Abroad will presently be forgotten, but this will survive. Don't be ashamed; don't be afraid. Leave the command in your will that your heirs shall put on your tombstone these words, and these alone: 'He wrote the immortal 1601.'" To be sure, though this is in some deeper sense finally serious, it is ironic as well; and the irony is further compounded by the fact that before his tragic death in a train accident, Gray had changed so utterly in his basic beliefs that he would have recanted his words of praise.

Though Gray, a poet and the editor of the *Buffalo Daily Courier*, rival of Twain's *Buffalo Express*, had been born into "a Presbyterianism of the bluest, the most uncompromising and unlovely shade," Twain recounts in another part of the autobiography, "When I was comrading with him, the Presbyterianism had all gone and he had become a frank rationalist and pronounced unbeliever"; but by the time of their final encounter, "his unbelief had all passed away." Nonetheless, Twain is still able to say of him that "he was great and fine, blemishless in character, a creature to adore." It seems to me that in any event it was Gray's hyperbolic praise that started Twain thinking about producing a larger, authorized edition of *1601*.

What finally made it possible, however, was his chance encounter with Lieutenant Charles Erskine Scott Wood, who was adjutant to the commanding general when in 1881, Twain — accompanied by Joe Twichell — made a visit to West Point. There he discovered not only that Wood, like him, was a freethinker, but that he had at his disposal a well-equipped printing plant. Shortly after returning home, Wood later reported, Twain wrote him a letter asking if he would be willing "to print a small thing he had written." This turned out to be, of course, *1601*, after reading which, Wood enthusiastically assented. He was intrigued, first of all, on political grounds, because the pious censors he hated would have found it "obscene"; but on aesthetic ones, too. That is to say, being well versed in the plastic arts as well as the verbal ones, he was able to see ways in which the pseudo-archaics of Twain's mock Elizabethan language could be reinforced typographically.

"I wrote Mark," he recalled, "that for literary effect there should be a species of forgery, though of course there was no effort to actually deceive a scholar." To this Twain responded "that I might do as I liked; — that his only object was to secure a number of copies, as the demand for it was becoming burdensome." Finally, after editing the spelling and diction of Twain's text a little, Wood printed, on deckle-edge vellum dampened with mild coffee to suggest age, and using Old English–style type, fifty copies of what Twain referred to later as "the sumptuous West Point edition."

In light of the fact that Wood was what Shakespeare would have called "the onlie begetter" of *1601*, it is odd that these days he seems to have been forgotten by almost everyone, including many Twain scholars. His name is not listed, for instance, in the indexes even of books which deal at some length with that "obscene" work, like Charles Neider's edition of the autobiography or Walter Blair's *Mark Twain and Huck Finn*. Yet in his own time, Wood was widely known to both academics and the general public; since after leaving the army he had achieved considerable success as an artist, a poet, an essayist, a lawyer, a politician — and especially as a gadfly to self-righteous defenders of the status quo and a champion of persecuted rebels, like Margaret Sanger, Emma Goldman and the anarcho-syndicalists of the IWW.

Mark Twain himself seems to have forgotten Wood in later years, making no mention of his name in his notebooks or his autobiography. Wood, on the other hand, never forgot Twain, though he outlived him by thirty-five years, dying at the age of ninety-two. He makes Twain, in fact, a major character in his *Heavenly Discourse*, which was not published until 1927. An attack on hypocritical piety and false patriotism, this book takes the form of conversations carried on in a kind of post-Christian, multicultural Heaven, the participants including not just Twain but Buddha, Lao Tzu, Rabelais, Voltaire, Satan, Jesus Christ and God Himself. Twain is starred, as seems appropriate considering the occasion for their brief relationship, in a couple of dialogues on obscenity — in one of which he is portrayed as saying, "Nature from manure brings flowers and fruits. It might be that by the same wonderful alchemy she should make from obscenity something vital and fine."

What explains Wood's consequent obscurity is surely, at least in part, the equivocal status of that nearly anonymous "obscene" book over whose production he presided. Unlike most of Twain's other later books, *1601* does not include in its front matter a portrait of the author, nor does his name appear on the title page. Also uncharacteristically, it was never sold — being, indeed, the only one of his works from which Twain never made a cent. But this is fair enough, since — as Twain wrote in 1906 to an inquisitive librarian — he never considered it a true sibling to his more legitimate books, describing it as a "Wandering offspring" which "I hasten to assure you is *not* printed in my published writing." Taking a cue from Twain, subsequent editors have excluded it from his collected works (the present volume and the Library of America's *Collected Tales, Sketches, Speeches, and Essays* excepted).

It seems to me, however, that *1601* can only be properly understood in the context of Twain's total oeuvre. Placing it in that setting makes clear how much this presumably unique book has in common with what critics consider his more characteristic ones. First of all, it deals with life in a foreign land, like so many other books by this most American of all American writers, beginning with his first, *The Innocents Abroad*, and continuing on until his unfinished last one, *The Mysterious Stranger*. But it takes us on a vicarious journey through time as well as space; and in this it resembles not just that full-fledged time-travel fantasy, *A Connecticut Yankee in King Arthur's Court*, but also the Tom Sawyer–Huck Finn series, with its almost magical resurrection of endless summers in an antebellum mid-America, otherwise presumably lost forever.

Finally, too, in this wider context it is possible to see *1601* as one of Twain's many linguistic experiments — to which he was driven, I think, though he may not have been fully conscious of it himself, by a need to escape the restrictions of what Victorians considered a proper literary dialect. Sometimes he sought, as in *A Connecticut Yankee* and *The Prince and the Pauper*, to do this by counterfeiting archaic speech; sometimes, as in *Huckleberry Finn*, by attempting to reproduce in writing oral colloquial dialects. In *1601*, he combines both strategies, interlarding the high diction of the Elizabethan court with the gross four-letter words which were then used solely in barrooms, back alleys — and, of course, pornography.

Even considered as pornography, however, *1601* does not stand alone among Twain's works. In addition to jotting down the punch lines of dirty jokes in his notebooks, he wrote for the eyes of men only raunchy poems like "The Mammoth Cod," and to a similar audience he made speeches like the notorious defense of masturbation delivered at the Stomach Club in Paris. Moreover, even in works intended for family reading, he flirted with taboos. So, for instance, in *Tom Sawyer* he discreetly describes Becky peeking at nude pictures in her teacher's anatomy book; and in *Huckleberry Finn* circumspectly hints at the phallic nature of the play put on by the Duke and the King for the yokels of a one-horse town in Arkansas.

Yet even at its hardest, Twain's pornography differs from the run-of-the-mill erotic literature whose popularity was peaking at the moment he wrote *1601*. In *The Other Victorians*, Steven Marcus argues that this popular genre was typically distinguished by three things. First, it is only "minimally verbal," which is to say, it tends to make its readers oblivious to rather than conscious of the language in which it is written. Second, it avoids defining specifically the time and place of its action. Third, its characters are invariably young, since its essential fable is a projection of the male fantasy of potency, in which the penis is imagined to be "a magical instrument of infinite powers."

But *1601*, as we have already observed, is conspicuously verbal. Moreover, its time and place are specified in the very title; and many of its characters are old, most notably the aged narrator and the Queen herself, who is at the date of the action sixty-eight. Finally, when it ceases to be basically scatological, as it is from the start, and becomes fully erotic, the male fantasy it projects is not the dream of infinite potency but the complementary nightmare of genital inadequacy, as is made clear by its mournful last line, ". . . which doing, lo hys member felle, & wolde not rise again."

In the end, *1601* is not only truly American but, like much of Twain's other writing, autobiographical. Of this Sir Walter Raleigh has earlier made us aware, telling of "a people in ye most uttermost parts of America that copulate not until they be five-&-thirty yeeres of age . . . & doe it then but once in seven yeeres"; (vi) thus leaving us to remember, as we close the book, that it was approximately at this age that Mark Twain married — for all his foul mouth, probably still a virgin.

2

Despite its misleading title, *Is Shakespeare Dead?* deals not with the problem of the poet's mortality but with that of his identity. It attempts, that is to say, to answer the question of who really wrote the works attributed to the actor from Stratford, and should therefore more properly have been called *Is "Shakespeare" Shakespeare?* But death was much on Twain's mind when he wrote this little book in 1909. He was still mourning his favorite daughter, Susy, who had been dead for more than a dozen years, and his beloved wife, Livy, who had been dead for five.

Moreover, the death of another daughter, Jean, lay just ahead, as did his own. The latter, at least, he must have foreseen, since his health was failing rapidly; and Halley's Comet, which had flashed across the sky when he was born — and to which he felt bound like a Siamese twin — was due to appear again the following year. It is scarcely strange, then, that the word "dead" intruded into the title of what was to be one of the last of his books published during his lifetime. What is strange, however, is that the text which follows is not melancholy but basically blithe and even at its most irascible moments punctuated with jokes. Indeed, it finally seems as if the mortuary title itself might be just another joke.

After all, we remember, in Twain's first book, *The Innocents Abroad,* he recounts how he and some irreverent fellow travelers would annoy their guides by asking a question "which never failed to disgust [them]." "We use it always when we can think of nothing else to say," he explains. "After they have exhausted their enthusiasm pointing out to us . . . the beauties of some bronze image . . . we look at it stupidly and in silence for . . . as long as we can hold out . . . and then ask, 'Is — is he dead?'" It seems reasonable that by playing the same game with the Shakespeare idolaters more than four decades later, Twain was able to imagine himself once more a "bad boy," challenging the cultural clichés of his elders.

But he was, of course, in reality a lonely old man, haunted by bad dreams and incapable of finishing any of the fictions in which he thought by embodying them to exorcise them. Only fragments survive of these nightmarish fantasies in which the terrified protagonist is shrunk and trapped in a drop of water, frozen into the eternal ice of the Arctic, overwhelmed by impenetrable darkness or blinded by intolerable light. The most nearly successful of such abortive ventures is the posthumously published pseudo-text called *The Mysterious Stranger*. Cobbled together and shamelessly emended (without acknowledgement) by Frederick Duneka and Albert Paine, this account of an ambiguously satanic figure who ends by revealing to the young man he has bedeviled that all he has taken as reality is "a grotesque and foolish dream" has come to be accepted not just as one of Twain's major works but as his final word to the world.

Yet though Twain was apparently working to the very end of his life on one or another of its three or four incoherent versions, it is not in fact his valedictory statement. Disconcertingly, that was *Is Shakespeare Dead?* — one of his least well received and most misunderstood works. Part of the problem, surely, is that this little book seems at first glance to belong to a genre which Twain did not customarily write, and not very successfully when he did: literary criticism.

His recorded comments on what he called "belles lettres" are few and far between. His preferred reading was popular history, philosophy and theology; and when he did try to read poetry and fiction it was at the urging of his friend and mentor William Dean Howells, who never ceased trying to induct him into the mysteries of high culture. Typically, however, Twain's responses were negative, brief and in any case intended for Howells' eyes only. Snidely and in few words, for instance, he dismissed both Edgar Allan Poe and Jane Austen, declaring, "To me his prose is unreadable — like [hers]. No, there is a difference. I could read his prose on salary, but not Jane's. Jane is entirely impossible. It seems a pity they allowed her to die a natural death." With almost equal brutality and brevity, he disposed of three other canonical authors, confessing, "I can't stand George Eliot & Hawthorne & those people; I see what they are at, a hundred years before they get to it, & they just tire me to death. And as for the Bostonians, I would rather be damned to John Bunyan's heaven than read that."

Only three times before his essay on Shakespeare appeared did Twain write about literature at greater length. Two of these essays, "Fenimore Cooper's Literary Offences" and "In Defense of Harriet Shelley," were published in the 1890s; the third, "William Dean Howells," not until 1906. The last of these differs from the other two as well as from Twain's brief epistolary comments, being overwhelmingly positive in tone. But this is scarcely surprising, since it is less objective criticism than a token of gratitude to one who even before they became friends had favorably reviewed Twain's work. In any event, Twain seems to have felt the piece inappropriate to the persona called by his nom de plume, whose function it was to mock everything admired by the respectable and conventional — including high literature. He therefore, uncharacteristically, published it under the name S. L. Clemens.

But "Mark Twain" was the name under which he issued what is surely the best known and most often reprinted of his critical essays, "Fenimore Cooper's Literary Offences" (1895). As a matter of fact, school dropout and autodidact that he was, he signed it "Mark Twain, M.A., Professor of Belles Lettres in the Veterinary College of Arizona." For a while, moreover, he tried to maintain a proper academic tone; but what begins as a patient *explication de texte* detailing Cooper's lapses in taste and style quickly degenerates into slander and calumny. "Cooper hadn't any more invention than a horse," he writes at one point, "and I don't mean a high-class horse, either; I mean a clothes-horse."

What prompts the most extravagant of these outbursts is not Cooper's literary ineptitude but the failure of certain self-styled experts to notice it. To make this clear, Twain prefixes to his essay what he considers particularly wrongheaded laudatory comments on Cooper by Professor Lounsbury of Yale, Professor Brander Matthews of Columbia and the British novelist Wilkie Collins; and then he observes scornfully, "It seems to me that it was far from right . . . to deliver opinions on Cooper's literature without having read some of it." In any case, what Twain is writing here is not criticism of literature but criticism of criticism — criticism twice removed; and so, too, is his earlier literary polemic against Shelley, published in 1894.

"In Defence of Harriet Shelley," as its title indicates, is primarily a chivalrous attempt to redeem the reputation of that ill-fated lady from what Twain felt to be the unfair representation of her in Professor Edward Dowden's *Life of Shelley*. He was, of course, irked by the good professor's bland assertion that despite having abandoned Harriet and run off with young Mary Godwin, Percy could not be held responsible for Harriet's suicide. But what seems especially to have enraged him was what he had apparently learned when his daughter Susy enrolled in Bryn Mawr, that Dowden's book was "accepted in the girls' colleges of America and its view taught in their literary classes."

To rebut Dowden, Twain not only attempts to reconstruct the true history of the relationship which Dowden falsified; he also tries to demonstrate the falsity of the rhetoric with which Dowden did so. Ironically enough, as he makes his case, his own rhetoric grows ever more hyperbolic and shrill. "The Shelley biography," he writes, "is a literary cake-walk. . . . all the pages . . . walk by . . . mincingly in their Sunday best. . . . It is rare to find a sentence that has forgotten to dress." This metaphor, he informs us, is drawn from the folk culture of "our Negroes in America." But once into the sort of adversarial criticism of criticism he relished, he draws on white high culture as well, telling us that Dowden's biography is "a Frankenstein with the original infirmity supplemented by a new one; a Frankenstein with the reasoning faculty wanting." This, too, is ironic enough, since the metaphor is drawn from the famous book by the second Mrs. Shelley; but the irony is twice compounded by the fact that Twain does not properly remember her book, confusing her nameless monster with its maker.

What had become evident by 1895, in any case, was that typically Twain was moved to write about literature only when his temper was aroused by critical opinions contrary to his own — especially if those opinions were propagated by academics. Thus, it seemed inevitable that sooner or later he would get mad enough to take sides in the ongoing controversy about the authorship of the poems and plays traditionally attributed to "William Shakespeare." Moreover, there seemed little doubt about which side he would support, since the scholars and critics who have determined the canon of Shakespeare's works, as well as edited and commented on them, have by and large ended up believing that their true author is the actor from Stratford.

Yet there has always been a minority of nonbelievers; and there are indeed few of us who are not a little disturbed by the fact that justly or unjustly, among the acknowledged greater writers of the world, Shakespeare is the only one whose identity has been thus challenged over and over. The person who seems to me to have come closest to explaining why is Wyndham Lewis, who in *The Lion and the Fox* wrote, "That there is something equivocal and of a very special nature in the figure of this poet has been felt constantly; and people have always tapped his pedestal, inquisitive and uneasy, peered up into his face, scenting hoax. The authenticity of that face has even been doubted; it has been called 'an obvious mask,' the 'face of a tailor's dummy.'"

When it comes to saying who was the real author, however, there has been widespread disagreement among the anti-Shakespeareans. Francis Bacon has been suggested, and Anthony Bacon; the Earl of Oxford and a host of other earls; Sir Walter Raleigh, Christopher Marlowe, Queen Elizabeth and even a nun called Anne Whatley. Francis Bacon, of course, is the all-time favorite — as he was Mark Twain's; though Twain could not quite bring himself to endorse him when he finally got around to addressing the Bacon-Shakespeare controversy in 1909. To be sure, he claims in *Is Shakespeare Dead?* that he had "a fifty years interest in the matter — born of Delia Bacon's book — away back on that ancient day — 1857, or maybe 1856." But there is no evidence of this in anything he published earlier.

He had, it is true, kept working throughout his career on a burlesque version of *Hamlet*, in which a kibitzer from the nineteenth century breaks into the action of the play. But though this makes it clear that Twain always wanted in some sense to make Shakespeare his own, nowhere does the manuscript betray the slightest doubt about that playwright's identity. Nor does *1601*, which includes both Shakespeare and Bacon in its cast of characters. In fact, in it Bacon is described not as a poet, actual or potential, but as "a tedious sink of learning" [who will] "ponderously philosophize" though "ye subject bee but a fart." On the other hand, "ye famous Shaxpur" is portrayed as reciting verses from *King Henry IV* and *Venus and Adonis*, whose authorship no one challenges, instead bestowing on him "prodigious admiration."

Nonetheless, by 1909 Twain had somehow persuaded himself that his skepticism about Shakespeare dated back half a century and had only been "asleep for the last three years." But he had, as is well known, an immense capacity for self-deceit, so that in this case, as in so many others, the real truth is hard to determine. Probably he really had, as he claims, supported the anti-Stratfordian position back in 1858, in a continuing half-earnest debate with George Ealer, the master pilot to whom he was then apprenticed, and a passionate pro-Stratfordian. But later, with no living opponent to combat, he seems to have lost all interest.

What revived it, apparently, was the chance arrival on his desk of the galleys of a book on Bacon by William S. Booth, which then led him to read George Greenwood's *The Shakespeare Problem Restated*, whose anti-Stratfordian arguments he echoes in *Is Shakespeare Dead?* — even quoting a large section of it verbatim. His enthusiasm he shared with his daughter Jean, telling her, "I am having a good time dictating to a stenographer a day-after-day scoff at everybody who is ignorant enough and stupid enough to go on believing that Shakespeare ever wrote a poem or play in his life." Clearly what pleased him was the opportunity to calumniate once more the kind of scholarly "experts" he had always despised, this time the historians and biographers whom he calls "these Stratfordolators, these Shakesperiods, these thugs, these bangalores, these troglodytes, these herumfrodites, these blatherskites, these buccaneers, these bandoleers. . ." (133–34).

No one else, however, was convinced. Albert Paine, who usually praised uncritically whatever he wrote, was so dubious that Twain felt obliged to reassure him, falsely claiming, "I have private knowledge from a source that cannot be questioned. It is the great discovery of the age." But the finished book contained nothing except a rehash of old arguments about the Stratford Shakespeare's lack of schooling and legal expertise — interlarded with outbursts of vitriolic abuse. Even Isabel Lyon, who after Livy's death was

Twain's closest female companion, felt forced to confess that it was "not gentle and not very clever"; agreeing therefore with other of his concerned friends that he was "slipping intellectually," and that it would be wise "*not to have his ideas made public.*"

In fact, his publishers finally issued the book only because they were contractually obligated to do so; and as they had foreseen, it received perfunctory notice in the press. One reviewer, trying to beat Twain at his own game, jocularly argued that since, like Shakespeare, he was an autodidact and school dropout, the literary works attributed to him must have been written by somebody else — probably Elbert Hubbard. Even those most deeply involved in the Shakespeare-Bacon controversy did not pay his book much heed. The only response of Greenwood himself, for instance, was a threat to sue Twain for inadequately acknowledging his borrowings. Naturally, with members of the critical establishment, to whom the "Baconian heresy" seemed as absurdly illusory as a belief in UFOs or Bigfoot, *Is Shakespeare Dead?* fared even less well. Typical is its dismissal in a recent Twain handbook intended for classroom use, which describes it as "an exaggerated pitch of a travelling salesman . . . repetitive, sporadic, and totally without direction . . . full of overblown, bombastic pseudo-eloquence."

It is a judgment with which it is hard to disagree if *Is Shakespeare Dead?* is read solely as an inept attempt at literary criticism. But after all, as its subtitle indicates, it is a piece "from my autobiography"; and only by keeping this in mind is it possible to perceive the sense in which it is finally coherent. We must, however, be aware of Twain's unorthodox notion that the right way to do an autobiography was "to wander at your free will all over your life; talk only about the thing which interests you at the moment; drop it the moment its interest threatens to pale." But this means that what pattern it has is unconscious, like that of a reverie or a dream.

Certainly, this is true of *Is Shakespeare Dead?*, which, despite its presumed subject, begins with an apparently irrelevant discourse on "claimants": pretenders of various kinds, including not just Mary Baker Eddy and Louis XVII but (rather astonishingly) the Golden Calf and Satan. To be sure, Shakespeare is mentioned as a "claimant," too, but only in passing; and before Twain manages to treat him at length, he has wandered off into reminiscences about his days as a riverboat pilot and the death on the river of his brother Henry. This in turn somehow segues into a not quite credible anecdote about his days in Sunday school and an explanation of his lifelong interest in Satan.

What is not clear, until he approaches the end of the book, is why Twain started it with the incantatory repetition of the word "claimants." At that point, he reminds us of the pilot's cry "m-a-rk-*twain*," which indicates safe water but is also his nom de plume; and we realize that "claimants," too, is a pun, this time on his given name, "Clemens." Finally, in what he calls a "postscript," he reproduces a clipping from a current edition of his hometown newspaper which identifies him as "Mark Twain or S. L. Clemens as a few of the unlettered call him": thus not merely joining together both of his names, but ironically reversing their claim to authenticity.

Between his two encrypted signatures, Twain not only piles up proof for his anti-Stratfordian brief; but — like a proper autobiographer — tells us much about his own early life. Indeed, if all other records were to disappear, we would know from *Is Shakespeare Dead?* not just when and where Twain was born, when his father died and he left school, but also what trades he practiced before he became a full-time writer and where they took him. Of his later life, however, he tells us little (not even mentioning his wife or daughters, for instance), only that he ended up by being everywhere in the world, but especially in his hometown, honored and loved — his name a byword.

This, he insists, is quite different from the ultimate fate of the pretender from Stratford, remembered and mourned by none of his fellow citizens — his very name forgotten. But why, I am moved to ask, does Twain not merely insist on that difference but feel a need to cite objective evidence to prove it. Could it be that somewhere below the level of full consciousness he had doubts about the identity not just of England's greatest writer but of one he needed desperately to believe was America's greatest, namely, himself — whoever he really was, Mark Twain? or S. L. Clemens? or both? or neither?

Certainly, throughout his writing life he had been obsessed by that question: making the confusion of identities the thematic center of *The Prince and the Pauper* and *Pudd'nhead Wilson*, and ending *Huckleberry Finn* with Huck taken for Tom and Tom not sure who he is supposed to be. His own personal identity crisis, which he projected in those fictional ones, is more clearly revealed in the famous "Whittier Birthday Speech," whose true significance has tended to be lost in subsequent analysis of the question of whether or not that speech scandalized the Boston Brahmins before whom Twain delivered it one ill-fated night in December of 1877.

The somewhat raunchy tale which Twain told in that inappropriate setting deals with a miner whose hospitality has been abused by three drunken louts impersonating three of those Brahmins, Emerson, Longfellow and Oliver Wendell Holmes. But as Twain observed some years later, he could as easily have had them call themselves Beaumont, Ben Jonson and Shakespeare; since the real point of the story is the plight of the first-person narrator, who arrives at the miner's cabin just after the three hooligans have departed.

After hearing the miner's story, that narrator, who has begun his own story by informing us, "I resolved to try the virtue of my *nom de plume*," explains that those other "littery" men were only imposters; to which the miner replies, "Ah — imposters, were they? — are *you*?" Small wonder, then, that some thirty years later Twain dreamed that he appeared at a "social gathering" dressed only in his nightshirt, and when he declared, "I am Mark Twain," no one believed him. Surely, it must have been just such a dream that he was dreaming in the three years' sleep from which he woke to write *Is Shakespeare Dead?*

FOR FURTHER READING

Leslie A. Fiedler

Because of its equivocal status in the Mark Twain canon, *1601* has not been treated at full length by any critic or scholar. Those who have dealt with it at all have done so cursorily and in passing. So, for instance, I myself did in an essay called "More Images of Eros and Old Age," which appeared in 1986 in *Memory and Desire*, a collection of gerontological studies edited by Kathleen Woodward and Murray Schwartz. Similarly, Walter Blair devotes a few pages to it in *Mark Twain and Huck Finn* (1960), since it was written at a moment when Twain had reached an impasse in the composition of the major novel which is Blair's chief concern.

Readers interested in further exploring the significance of *1601* and its place in Twain's total oeuvre will find scattered information in other sources. Some of the privately printed editions are usefully annotated, particularly the one edited by Franklin J. Maine and published in Chicago in 1959 under the auspices of the Mark Twain Society. Biographical sources are another possibility; first of all, of course, Twain's autobiography, both as it was edited early on by Albert B. Paine (1924) and later as reedited and augmented by Charles Neider (1959). Additional background material is to be found in biographies, both the first one, also written by Paine (1912), and those based on subsequent research, like Justin Kaplan's *Mr. Clemens and Mark Twain* (1966) and Hamlin Hill's *Mark Twain: God's Fool* (1973).

Such sources cast light, too, on *Is Shakespeare Dead?*, particularly, of course, Paine's biography, since he was Twain's close companion and confidant during the time that book was being written. There is, moreover, a full-length study of it (as well as a typically brief commentary on *1601*) in Anthony J. Berret's *Mark Twain and Shakespeare*, published in 1993. Some of the same ground was covered earlier — as Berret duly acknowledges — in "Is Shakespeare Dead? Mark Twain's Irreverent Question," an essay by Thomas J. Richardson which appeared in 1985 in *Shakespeare and Southern Writers*, edited by Philip C. Kolin.

Richardson had in turn acknowledged his indebtedness to Alan Gribben's *Mark Twain's Library: A Reconstruction* (1980) and Howard G. Baetzhold's *Mark Twain and John Bull* (1970), both of which contribute to a fuller understanding of Twain's uses of Shakespeare in *1601* and *Is Shakespeare Dead?* by setting them in the context of his knowledge of and attitude toward the literary high culture of England as a whole.

A NOTE ON THE TEXT

Robert H. Hirst

The text of *Date 1601. Conversation, as it was by the Social Fireside, in the time of the Tudors* is a photographic facsimile of the first authorized American edition (known as the West Point edition) dated 1882 on the title page. This edition of 50 copies was privately printed from Mark Twain's manuscript (now lost) by Charles Erskine Scott Wood at the United States Military Academy at West Point, New York (*BAL* 3407). Mark Twain sent Wood the manuscript on April 3, 1882, and the printing was completed by July 14. The copy reproduced here is a signed presentation copy to George Iles (1852–1942), a friend of Clemens' who was manager of the Windsor Hotel in Montreal. The original is in the collection of the Harry Ransom Humanities Research Center at the University of Texas at Austin (PS1322/S45/ 1882/ HRC). §The text of *Is Shakespeare Dead? from My Autobiography* is a photographic facsimile of a copy of the first American edition, all known copies of which are dated 1909 on the title page. The first edition was published in April 1909; two copies were deposited with the Copyright Office on April 8. The copy reproduced here is an example of Jacob Blanck's first issue (*BAL* 3509). The original volume is in the collection of the Mark Twain House in Hartford, Connecticut (810/C625is/1909/c. 1).

The Mark Twain House is a museum and research center dedicated to the study of Mark Twain, his works, and his times. The museum is located in the nineteen-room mansion in Hartford, Connecticut, built for and lived in by Samuel L. Clemens, his wife, and their three children, from 1874 to 1891. The Picturesque Gothic-style residence, with interior design by the firm of Louis Comfort Tiffany and Associated Artists, is one of the premier examples of domestic Victorian architecture in America. Clemens wrote *Adventures of Huckleberry Finn*, *The Adventures of Tom Sawyer*, *A Connecticut Yankee in King Arthur's Court*, *The Prince and the Pauper*, and *Life on the Mississippi* while living in Hartford.

The Mark Twain House is open year-round. In addition to tours of the house, the educational programs of the Mark Twain House include symposia, lectures, and teacher training seminars that focus on the contemporary relevance of Twain's legacy. Past programs have featured discussions of literary censorship with playwright Arthur Miller and writer William Styron; of the power of language with journalist Clarence Page, comedian Dick Gregory, and writer Gloria Naylor; and of the challenges of teaching *Adventures of Huckleberry Finn* amidst charges of racism.

CONTRIBUTORS

Leslie A. Fiedler is the author of more than twenty-five books, including *An End to Innocence* (1955), *Love and Death in the American Novel* (1960), *Freaks: Myths and Images of the Secret Self* (1977), *What Was Literature?* (1982), and *Fiedler on the Roof: Essays on Literature and Jewish Identity* (1991). Widely known for his provocative interpretations of American literature and for his passionate devotion to a nonelitist view of popular culture, he has received numerous honors for his criticism and fiction, and has lectured all over the world. He is Samuel Clemens Professor of English at the State University of New York at Buffalo.

Shelley Fisher Fishkin, professor of American Studies and English at the University of Texas at Austin, is the author of the award-winning books *Was Huck Black? Mark Twain and African-American Voices* (1993) and *From Fact to Fiction: Journalism and Imaginative Writing in America* (1985). Her most recent book is *Lighting Out for the Territory: Reflections on Mark Twain and American Culture* (1996). She holds a Ph.D. in American Studies from Yale University, has lectured on Mark Twain in Belgium, England, France, Israel, Italy, Mexico, the Netherlands, and Turkey, as well as throughout the United States, and is president-elect of the Mark Twain Circle of America.

Robert H. Hirst is the General Editor of the Mark Twain Project at The Bancroft Library, University of California in Berkeley. Apart from that, he has no other known eccentricities.

Erica Jong, a novelist, poet, and essayist, holds a B.A. from Barnard College and an M.A. in eighteenth-century English literature from Columbia University. Her novels include *Fear of Flying* (1973), *How to Save Your Own Life* (1977), *Fanny: Being the True History of the Adventures of Fanny Hack-about-Jones* (1980), *Parachutes and Kisses* (1984), *Serenissima* (or *Shylock's Daughter*, 1987), and *Any Woman's Blues* (1990); among her books of poetry are *Fruits and Vegetables* (1971), *Half-Lives* (1973),

Loveroot (1975), *At the Edge of the Body* (1979), and *Becoming Light: Poems New and Selected* (1992). Her poems were recorded as songs on the album *Zipless* by Vanessa Daou. She is also the author of *The Devil at Large* (1993), a study of Henry Miller, and *Fear of Fifty* (1994). Her reviews and essays have appeared all over the world as have her novels, nonfiction, and poetry. Ms. Jong lives in New York City and Connecticut. She is currently at work on a new novel.

ACKNOWLEDGMENTS

There are a number of people without whom The Oxford Mark Twain would not have happened. I am indebted to Laura Brown, senior vice president and trade publisher, Oxford University Press, for suggesting that I edit an "Oxford Mark Twain," and for being so enthusiastic when I proposed that it take the present form. Her guidance and vision have informed the entire undertaking.

Crucial as well, from the earliest to the final stages, was the help of John Boyer, executive director of the Mark Twain House, who recognized the importance of the project and gave it his wholehearted support.

My father, Milton Fisher, believed in this project from the start and helped nurture it every step of the way, as did my stepmother, Carol Plaine Fisher. Their encouragement and support made it all possible. The memory of my mother, Renée B. Fisher, sustained me throughout.

I am enormously grateful to all the contributors to The Oxford Mark Twain for the effort they put into their essays, and for having been such fine, collegial collaborators. Each came through, just as I'd hoped, with fresh insights and lively prose. It was a privilege and a pleasure to work with them, and I value the friendships that we forged in the process.

In addition to writing his fine afterword, Louis J. Budd provided invaluable advice and support, even going so far as to read each of the essays for accuracy. All of us involved in this project are greatly in his debt. Both his knowledge of Mark Twain's work and his generosity as a colleague are legendary and unsurpassed.

Elizabeth Maguire's commitment to The Oxford Mark Twain during her time as senior editor at Oxford was exemplary. When the project proved to be more ambitious and complicated than any of us had expected, Liz helped make it not only manageable, but fun. Assistant editor Elda Rotor's wonderful help in coordinating all aspects of The Oxford Mark Twain, along with literature editor T. Susan Chang's enthusiastic involvement with the project in its final stages, helped bring it all to fruition.

I am extremely grateful to Joy Johannessen for her astute and sensitive copyediting, and for having been such a pleasure to work with. And I appreciate the conscientiousness and good humor with which Kathy Kuhtz Campbell heroically supervised all aspects of the set's production. Oxford president Edward Barry, vice president and editorial director Helen McInnis, marketing director Amy Roberts, publicity director Susan Rotermund, art director David Tran, trade editorial, design and production manager Adam Bohannon, trade advertising and promotion manager Woody Gilmartin, director of manufacturing Benjamin Lee, and the entire staff at Oxford were as supportive a team as any editor could desire.

The staff of the Mark Twain House provided superb assistance as well. I would like to thank Marianne Curling, curator, Debra Petke, education director, Beverly Zell, curator of photography, Britt Gustafson, assistant director of education, Beth Ann McPherson, assistant curator, and Pam Collins, administrative assistant, for all their generous help, and for allowing us to reproduce books and photographs from the Mark Twain House collection. One could not ask for more congenial or helpful partners in publishing.

G. Thomas Tanselle, vice president of the John Simon Guggenheim Memorial Foundation, and an expert on the history of the book, offered essential advice about how to create as responsible a facsimile edition as possible. I appreciate his very knowledgeable counsel.

I am deeply indebted to Robert H. Hirst, general editor of the Mark Twain Project at The Bancroft Library in Berkeley, for bringing his outstanding knowledge of Twain editions to bear on the selection of the books photographed for the facsimiles, for giving generous assistance all along the way, and for providing his meticulous notes on the text. The set is the richer for his advice. I would also like to express my gratitude to the Mark Twain Project, not only for making texts and photographs from their collection available to us, but also for nurturing Mark Twain studies with a steady infusion of matchless, important publications.

I would like to thank Jeffrey Kaimowitz, curator of the Watkinson Library at Trinity College, Hartford (where the Mark Twain House collection is kept), along with his colleagues Peter Knapp and Alesandra M. Schmidt, for having been instrumental in Robert Hirst's search for first editions that could be safely reproduced. Victor Fischer, Harriet Elinor Smith, and especially Kenneth M. Sanderson, associate editors with the Mark Twain Project, reviewed the note on the text in each volume with cheerful vigilance. Thanks are also due to Mark Twain Project associate editor Michael Frank and administrative assistant Brenda J. Bailey for their help at various stages.

I am grateful to Helen K. Copley for granting permission to publish photographs in the Mark Twain Collection of the James S. Copley Library in La Jolla, California, and to Carol Beales and Ron Vanderhye of the Copley Library for making my research trip to their institution so productive and enjoyable.

Several contributors — David Bradley, Louis J. Budd, Beverly R. David, Robert Hirst, Fred Kaplan, James S. Leonard, Toni Morrison, Lillian S. Robinson, Jeffrey Rubin-Dorsky, Ray Sapirstein, and David L. Smith — were particularly helpful in the early stages of the project, brainstorming about the cast of writers and scholars who could make it work. Others who participated in that process were John Boyer, James Cox, Robert Crunden, Joel Dinerstein, William Goetzmann, Calvin and Maria Johnson, Jim Magnuson, Arnold Rampersad, Siva Vaidhyanathan, Steve and Louise Weinberg, and Richard Yarborough.

Kevin Bochynski, famous among Twain scholars as an "angel" who is gifted at finding methods of making their research run more smoothly, was helpful in more ways than I can count. He did an outstanding job in his official capacity as production consultant to The Oxford Mark Twain, supervising the photography of the facsimiles. I am also grateful to him for having put me in touch via e-mail with Kent Rasmussen, author of the magisterial *Mark Twain A to Z*, who was tremendously helpful as the project proceeded, sharing insights on obscure illustrators and other points, and generously being "on call" for all sorts of unforeseen contingencies.

I am indebted to Siva Vaidhyanathan of the American Studies Program of the University of Texas at Austin for having been such a superb research assistant. It would be hard to imagine The Oxford Mark Twain without the benefit of his insights and energy. A fine scholar and writer in his own right, he was crucial to making this project happen.

Georgia Barnhill, the Andrew W. Mellon Curator of Graphic Arts at the American Antiquarian Society in Worcester, Massachusetts, Tom Staley, director of the Harry Ransom Humanities Research Center at the University of Texas at Austin, and Joan Grant, director of collection services at the Elmer Holmes Bobst Library of New York University, granted us access to their collections and assisted us in the reproduction of several volumes of The Oxford Mark Twain. I would also like to thank Kenneth Craven, Sally Leach, and Richard Oram of the Harry Ransom Humanities Research Center for their help in making HRC materials available, and Jay and John Crowley, of Jay's Publishers Services in Rockland, Massachusetts, for their efforts to photograph the books carefully and attentively.

I would like to express my gratitude for the grant I was awarded by the University Research Institute of the University of Texas at Austin to defray some of the costs of researching The Oxford Mark Twain. I am also grateful to American Studies director Robert Abzug and the University of Texas for the computer that facilitated my work on this project (and to UT systems analyst Steve Alemán, who tried his best to repair the damage when it crashed). Thanks also to American Studies administrative assistant Janice Bradley and graduate coordinator Melanie Livingston for their always generous and thoughtful help.

The Oxford Mark Twain would not have happened without the unstinting, wholehearted support of my husband, Jim Fishkin, who went way beyond the proverbial call of duty more times than I'm sure he cares to remember as he shared me unselfishly with that other man in my life, Mark Twain. I am also grateful to my family — to my sons Joey and Bobby, who cheered me on all along the way, as did Fannie Fishkin, David Fishkin, Gennie Gordon, Mildred Hope Witkin, and Leonard, Gillis, and Moss

Plaine — and to honorary family member Margaret Osborne, who did the same.

My greatest debt is to the man who set all this in motion. Only a figure as rich and complicated as Mark Twain could have sustained such energy and interest on the part of so many people for so long. Never boring, never dull, Mark Twain repays our attention again and again and again. It is a privilege to be able to honor his memory with The Oxford Mark Twain.

Shelley Fisher Fishkin
Austin, Texas
April 1996